PUMA PISTOLEERS

Before the advent of the railroad, Puma Valley was open cow country, ramrodded by two big ranchers, Paul Malone and Pete Glenn. They didn't take too well to the small farmers who arrived on the train and staked claim to the land. So, with the Valley on the brink of war, the railroad hired young Cal Rutherford to protect the farmers. But it looked like nobody could save them from lawlessness. One by one, Malone and Glenn claimed their victims. Then a drought wiped out the crops. Finally, only Cal stood between the ruthless ranchers and the desperate new settlers, with his .45 and a will of steel.

LEE FLOREN

PUMA PISTOLEERS

Complete and Unabridged

LINFORD
Leicester

A-1

First Linford Edition
published February 1989

British Library CIP Data

Floren, Lee, *1910–*
    Puma pistoleers.—Large print ed.—
Linford western library
I. Title
813'.52[F]

ISBN 0-7089-6673-X

Published by
F. A. Thorpe (Publishing) Ltd.
Anstey, Leicestershire
Set by Rowland Phototypesetting Ltd.
Bury St. Edmunds, Suffolk
Printed and bound in Great Britain by
T. J. Press (Padstow) Ltd., Padstow, Cornwall

1

THE first thought, upon regaining consciousness, was that he had failed. And because he was only sixteen, and because this was his first job, he tasted the bitterness of defeat. Then his second thought was about Cal Rutherford.

Cal Rutherford would not be as angry as he would be disgusted. Cal was not the type who was quick to become angry. Cal had sent him out to the storage-bin after a load of wheat and he had let the four-horse team run away. And somebody had slugged him, too.

Dimly, memory returned. He had been ready to go down the grade, and he was stopping at the summit, for he had aimed to rough-lock his wagon wheels, since the grade down was steep. His two teams, strung out, had been lathered, for the up-grade had been a tough pull, with the grain-tank loaded with Montana wheat. He had been ready to swing down off the wagon when the man had slugged him.

His memory was clear now.

He looked around, his head aching as if a mule were inside his skull, kicking with steel-shod hoofs. He was down in the canyon. His shirt was half-torn from him, showing gaunt ribs scratched and bleeding from the tumble through the thorns of wild rose-bushes. He couldn't move his left leg. His right leg was all right—so were his arms—and he tried to stand up. He couldn't. His left leg wouldn't work. He went down again in the sandy bottom of the canyon, half-sitting, half-lying.

Nausea swam in on him, making his brain fuzzy.

He had been ready to swing down to make this rough-lock when the gun-barrel had descended. The man had come out of the brush behind the wagon, caught the end-gate and swung up. Then, moving silently, walking through the wheat in the load, he had come behind the boy, and then he had slugged.

He remembered trying to fight with the man, and he remembered the man had been masked. The gun had boomed down again and he was aware of other riders, roaring out of the high buckbrush, guns flaming. Useless shots pounding upward. But the roar had been enough.

He remembered the four horses lurching wildly ahead. Terrified, they had started down the steep road at a lope. The heavy wheat-tank had lurched, straightened, and then blackness had come to him.

But he remembered hearing, just before he passed out, the harsh voice of a man hollering, "Jump, fella, jump!"

That man had been advising the assailant to jump from the wagon. That had been the last he remembered. Somewhere, along that mad canyon run, he had been dumped from the wagon. Or had he gone over the lip with the wagon, the wheat, and the teams? He tried to get on his feet again.

His right hand braced against a sandstone, he got upright, putting his weight on his right leg. The pain in his left leg was like a white-hot iron. He gritted his teeth and stood there, trying to look down the canyon. But the buck-brush was high. Too high.

He was a thin youth, starting to stretch to manhood. Someday he would make a big man. But now, he was painly gaunt—he'd been underfed. He had long arms, and his wrists were beginning to thicken, but his face was not boyish—it was gaunt and the cheek-bones

3

protruded under the light down of his first whiskers. His levis were torn and dirty from his tumble down the canyon.

He thought, Cal won't be mad. But he will be disgusted.

To him, Cal Rutherford was almost a god. The month before, a freight had pulled, into Puma City, and it had picked up a carload of wheat at Cal Rutherford's elevator. Cal Rutherford and the conductor had walked down the train to see that the coupling had secured itself.

Then the conductor had seen him. "Get off this train, punk. Get off, I say, or I'll split your skull open!"

The kid had been dodging around the end of a box-car. The conductor had started after him with a billy-club. The kid had seen flight was useless; the conductor carried a gun. So the youth had stopped running. He stood beside Cal Rutherford, and Cal had seen the ugly defiance in the thin, sallow face.

"You try to hit me, conductor, and I'll kill you with my hands!"

The statement had been ironical. The conductor was mature and tough and outweighed him by sixty pounds or so. But the

4

conductor had stopped. Not because of fear, but because of surprise.

"I told you to get off this train in Wahpaton, kid. Now you stay off, an' I'll not bother you no more."

"You don't own this railroad."

"No, but I boss this train."

The kid had looked squarely at Cal Rutherford as if seeing him for the first time. "I'm ridin' west," he said. "I'm lookin' for a job, mister. Is there work for me in this town?"

"What kind of work?"

"Any kind of work where a man can make an honest buck, sir."

Cal Rutherford held back his smile. Cal was twenty-four and he'd known a big city as a youth, and he'd known privation. Something about this youth—his worn levis, his pinched face—stirred a memory in the young elevator-man. A memory that held no delight. . . .

Cal said, "I can use you, kid. What's your name?"

"Jimmy."

"Last name?"

Jimmy looked at his new boss. "Do you need to know?"

"Everybody just about has a last name." Cal

5

Rutherford spoke quietly. "That seems to be a habit, Jimmy."

Jimmy watched him. "All right, but I won't take my stepdad's name, even if he did have the court put it on me. Stephens is my last name."

Cal had looked at the conductor. "He's hired." The man hung his billy-club back on his belt. Cal told Jimmy to go over to the elevator and wait for him. This grain elevator was a novelty here in Montana. It raised its blunt snoot high into the air. It was the first grain elevator along this section of the railroad. Jimmy went toward Cal's office and Cal and the conductor continued down the train.

"You might regret that move," the conductor said. "That bum might lift your cash some night an' skeedaddle."

"I'll chance that."

There was a tone of finality in Cal Rutherford's voice. The conductor sent him a sharp glance, but said nothing. To him anybody who rode a freight was a bum and would never be anything but a bum. Jimmy had worked for Cal and worked hard. He'd loaded grain-cars with wheat, the dust thick in the car; he'd shovelled wheat when an elevator-bucket broke; he and Cal had become good friends.

Gradually the boy came to realize what a tough deal Cal Rutherford was bucking. For Cal was bringing farmers into Puma Valley. He was bringing in farmers who fenced land and ploughed up virgin sod.

For until the coming of the railroad, Puma Valley had been a big cow-country, with two big outfits running most of the cattle. Paul Malone, a red-faced, thick-shouldered Irishman, ran the Heart Circle. Heart Circle cattle ran on the north side of the valley, with Puma River as a mythical dividing line separating the Malone ranch from the graze of Pete Glenn, who ran the Bar N iron.

But with the railroad came young Cal Rutherford. Borrowing money from the railroad, he built his elevator. But an elevator is no good without wheat to load into box-cars. Still backed by railroad money—money on which he paid a terrible rate of interest—Cal brought in teams and broke a section of sod. This he planted into wheat.

Luck had been with him. His wheat had sprouted, then drought had set in—a drought luckily broken by a good rain that brought full heads to his wheat. His threshing machine had turned out lots of wheat. This he stored in granaries. He aimed to hold his wheat until prices went up.

That had been last year. That fall ten farmers came in, built cabins, and stuck through a hard cold winter. They were going to farm on shares for Cal who had, through the railroad, gotten a land concession. He had not been able to grub-stake them. Nor had he been able to buy farming implements for them. For the railroad had cut his funds short.

Although Cal Rutherford hadn't said much, Jimmy Stephens had seen his boss worry scrawled across a face that was losing its boyish look. The railroad was playing an old game. The officials had got Cal to do the heavy work —break the land, build the elevator, get in farmers, thresh the wheat. Now the land was worth something. They aimed to pinch in Cal's money-supply and take over his property. And besides, he would be deep in debt to the rail-road, even after the company took his property. And the summer heat was helping the railroad, too.

Wheat had sprouted and had a small rain. Now for five weeks it had been dry, with the sun deriding them from its safe retreat in a brassy hot sky. Wheat was dying: rain was needed. Rain that never seemed to come.

Besides, there was Paul Malone and Pete Glenn.

Jimmy had been sweeping out Cal's office that day that Paul Malone rode up, dismounted, ground-tied his bronc, and came inside. His red face was redder than the wattles of an angry rooster.

"Rutherford, my cattle got into one of the wheat-fields of one of your farmer's. Broke down the fence last night, he claims. He shot two of my choice cows. Then he run the rest out of open range."

"Who was the farmer?"

"Mack Larson."

Cal Rutherford stood up. "I'm awfully sorry, Malone. I was hopin' somethin' like this would never happen."

Paul Malone spoke bluntly. "This range ain't got no place for farmers, Rutherford. They tell me you used to work cattle down in Colorado. That bein' so, you know they ain't no place for farmers on this graze."

"I think you're wrong, Malone."

Paul Malone's eyes had bugged slightly. "I bin runnin' beef in Puma Valley for over twenty years. I'll be hard to push out. Ain't never said this before, 'cause my wife an' Edwina don't want no trouble, but trouble bumped into me when that farmer shot them two cows."

"I'll make him pay you for them."

"He still shot them," Malone stated.

Finally Malone had ridden off. Three days later Pete Glenn met Cal Rutherford on the street. "Farmers are hazin' my stock aroun'," the Bar N owner snapped. "They claim grass I've run on for years. Me, I'm not standin' for it, Rutherford. Tell your sodbusters that!"

"They're on land they legally own."

"They're on land I used to run cows on," Pete Glenn stated.

He was a tough gent, this Pete Glenn. Maybe he was forty, but if were, he looked younger. He was a dandy in dress. California pants with a nice crease, polished brown boots, silver-inlaid spurs, silver conchos on the bat-wings of his leather chaps. His face was blocky, set on a thick neck that blended into heavy shoulders. Now his light blue eyes were on Cal Rutherford.

"That's my range," Pete Glenn repeated.

Up to now, the two big cowmen had made no open signs of antagonism toward the sodbusters. But Cal Rutherford had known all the time neither Pete Glenn nor Paul Malone had wanted the farmers in. A plough and a fence killed open range. And cowmen needed open range to keep in business. The profit in the cow business was so small at present what with low-priced markets that a man couldn't afford to run cattle over land he had to pay taxes on.

Then there was the unwritten law in Montana —the law of the cattleman—and this unwritten law said, "Land you run cattle on, whether government land or not, is automatically your range." And Cal Rutherford, standing there, knew this law would soon clash with written law . . . and trouble would result.

But the farmers needed money. And Cal could get no more from railroad officials. So he had decided to sell his wheat. He had sent Jimmy out with the grain-tank and two-bronc teams strung out ahead of the big wagon.

"Take it easy, Jimmy."

"I sure will, Cal."

Pride had been in Jimmy Stephens as he had jogged his teams along the prairie road toward one of the small granaries. Lazy dust had lifted from under the hoofs of the horses and from under the wide steel rims of the wagon's wheels. And Jimmy had automatically looked at the sky.

No clouds in sight. Only the brassy, silent sun. And the heat. Loading the wagon had been hard work.

He had shovelled the grain into the big wagonbox. Shovelled it in with a grain-scoop. The grain-tank held almost one hundred and fifty bushels of wheat. He had spent the night at the granary, sleeping on the wheat with his teams picketed out along the creek.

Next day at dawn he had started out. The distance was almost twenty-five miles from the granary to Puma City. He rested his horses at, noon on Willow Creek. He had been going down the grade when he'd been slugged. His interest all on his teams and the steep descent ahead, he had not heard the man come up behind him, for the grain had muffled the man's boots.

Pain ran riot in his left leg. Still, it felt a little better. Was it broken? Panic held him momentarily, drawing a fine mist across his eyes. He put his head down and cried. But this did him no good. Where were his teams? Where was the grain-tank? Who had slugged him?

"Either one of them blasted cowmen!" He spoke the words aloud. They echoed back from the opposite rocks. "Either Paul Malone or Pete Glenn, they did it. They don't want Cal to sell his wheat. He'd have *dinero* then to back his farmers an' fight them cowmen."

His head ached, but he moved ahead slowly. By now, he could put a little weight on his bum leg—then it wasn't broken, he was sure. The pain was up in his hip. Still, it wouldn't bear his full weight.

How long had he lain in this canyon? He looked for the sun but it was already down behind the hills. Dusk was reaching purple fingers into the bowels of the canyon. He had been out quite a time. Where were his teams and the wagon? Had they gone down the grade, too?

He looked up at the grade, about a hundred feet above him. Then he saw the ruts made by the wagon as it had plunged off the grade. A sickening sensation was in him. If the wagon had stampeded off the grade, the teams had gone with it. Somewhere ahead would be ruins.

He could vision the wreckage. The big grain-tank, load spilled to hell and gone, smashed, wheels askew. And the teams? Horses would die down that steep fall. If not killed outright, they would suffer broken legs, anyway.

This would hit Cal Rutherford hard.

For a moment, blind despair tugged at Jimmy Stephens. Cal had trusted him and here he had—. He hobbled ahead, moving faster now. He came to a bend in the dry bed of the canyon. There, ahead, he saw the grain wagon.

The grain-tank lay on its side, wedged against a boulder. A scatteration of wheat lay in the wedge of its bottom. The rest of the wheat was scattered, dotting the trail down which the wagon had plunged.

Jimmy's first thought was, Well, that's ruined, and it's the only grain-tank Cal had, and his second thought was, But where are the broncs?

For no horses lay dead in the gully. The boy hobbled close, looked at the double-trees. Then it came to him. It came in a slow, lazy way, and it came with pain—for his head still ached terribly.

He reconstructed the scene in his mind's eye. The man had slugged him, the other had ridden out masked and stampeded the team, then the man who had slugged him had thrown him to one side, tossing him off the grain-tank. He had

14

then rolled through brush to the bottom of this canyon.

Then the man had dropped down onto the tongue of the plunging, heavy wagon. There had been slack and he had pulled the doubletree pins, thus freeing the teams. The teams had thundered on, the man climbing astraddle one bronc, and probably pulling the broncs to a slow halt.

But what about the wagon?

The wagon had plunged on. The tongue was snapped short. Jimmy knew the tongue had buried itself in the road, twisted, and thrown the wagon into the gully. The kid straightened, a vague relief in him.

Well, no broncs had been killed. Thank God for that. But where were the horses? Had the raiders stolen them?

He doubted this. A horsethief, even if he were a cowman, faced but one penalty here in Montana—death at the end of a rope. Maybe whoever had slugged him had just let the broncs go loose. If such was the case, they might go into town. There Cal would see his horses and come out to investigate.

There was nothing he could do here. He looked up at the grade, now dark with onrushing night. He would have to get up on the road. He would have to climb up there before full darkness came.

On hands and knees, his bum leg a definite liability, Jimmy Stephens started his long climb up that boulder-strewn shale hill. He got ten feet and then slipped, rapping his sore hip against a rock. This brought pain to him and sweat showed on his forehead.

He hardly remembered that climb. One memory stood clear: back east in grammar school, in one of their readers, there had been a story about a man in hell, and the story had been about his hard climb out of hell. He was climbing up out of hell. Not a red, roaring hell, but a hell of wreckage—the wreckage of a big grain-wagon. He slipped.

For a moment, he lay there. Then he was on his way again, clawing over shale, dragging his leg, digging in his good knee, seeking leverage. He was dogged now, and fear and pain were separate, two elements in him but elements he would not acknowledge.

He was, for some reason, surprised when he reached the top. The flat, dirty road was before him. The moon was up and he realized, in a detached manner, that it must have taken an

16

hour—yes, maybe more than an hour—to climb that slope. He lay in the road.

He could go no further.

Hope, at this moment, was thin in him. For nobody, he figured, would travel this road until tomorrow. It led to the farms. And the farmers would be doing their chores at this hour.

Perhaps a farmer had gone to town and would come home late and find him? That was a wild wish. If one or more of the sodbusters had driven into Puma City that day he or they would be home by now. For this was a treacherous road to travel after dark. And besides, the farmers would go home early to do chores.

He would probably be on this road until morning, anyway, before somebody came along. That thought was not pleasant. He looked around. At this point, the grain-wagon had gone over the lip of the gully.

The heavy wagon, plummeting down, had broken off a clump of diamond-willows. He crawled to the clump and found a stout cane. This helped him to his feet. He would hobble as far as he could.

At that, he went a mile. Suddenly he stopped, with hope warm in his belly. Had he heard the ring of a tug-chain up ahead? He listened, heart wild; he heard the ring of a wheel on the road.

His dry lips formed one word, "Luck."

He waited, leaning on his cane. Then out of the night came a buckboard, dim, uncertain. One man on the seat. The rig came closer and he saw the white streak of a bald-faced horse's head. That would be Cal's horse, Old Baldy!

"Cal!"

The rig stopped. "Who's there?"

Jimmy realized he was hidden by the shadow of a steep bank behind him. He hobbled ahead, almost forgetting his painful hip.

"Over here, Cal!"

2

THE light from the kerosene lamp was yellow against the walls of the small room. The rays seemed to concentrate on the boy who lay on the cot. Jimmy Stephens slept and the smell of chloroform was cloying on the still air.

"What do you say, Doc?"

Doc Wilson looked up at Cal Rutherford. "Near as I can determine, Cal, the hip isn't broken. During that fall he's twisted his leg and dislocated the hip-joint. We'll set it and keep him in bed a few days for observation."

Cal smiled. He was six feet and wiry, and he smiled easily.

"That's good news, Doc. Glad he ain't hurt no worse."

Doc Wilson spoke seriously. "It isn't Jimmy I'm worried about, Cal. I'm worried about you."

Cal nodded. He was silent. He knew what the medico was driving at. When that grain-tank went over the gully it signified the beginning of a range war. Not cowman against cowman, but cowmen against Carl Rutherford's farmers.

"I'll get by, Doc."

"Pete Glenn's in town," the medico said. "He's playin' cards down in the Down Ace, an' Marfa Jordan is along with him. Then they done told me Paul Malone is down at the hotel."

Cal said, "Don't worry."

The sudden harshness in the elevator-man's voice made Doc Wilson give him a quick look. Doc Wilson was an old-timer here on this range. He could feel and understand the moods of the cowmen and nesters. And this brought a slow sign to him as he said, "I might be busy in the next month or so. . . ."

Cal knew what the medico meant, too. Gunshot wounds. . . . Gunfights. . . . Maybe dead men. And Cal Rutherford's face was graven granite as he stood and looked down on Jimmy Stephens.

"Hope you're wrong, Doc."

Doc Wilson grunted something. He was neutral in this. His job was to take care of the sick and wounded and not try to avert a range war. He lifted the injured leg of the naked youth who slept with his mouth open.

"You take his shoulders, Cal. Hold him hard. I still think this leg is only out of joint."

Cal held the youth by the shoulders. The medico pulled the leg, got it extended and rigid, and twisted the foot slightly. "Not broken," he panted. "If it was broken, we could hear the bones grate." He pulled harder and twisted again, and Cal Rutherford heard the ball slip into the hip-socket. Then Doc Wilson, forehead suddenly sweaty, slowly lowered the leg to the bed.

"Just a dislocation, Cal."

Cal said, "He's young and wiry. He'll get along fast now." He was thinking of a canyon and a grain-tank—a grain-tank smashed and ruined, with wheat scattered all over. And Doc Wilson stood and watched him as the medico wiped his stubby fingers with a clean towel.

"Either Pete Glenn and his men, Doc—either Glenn or Paul Malone and his riders."

"That thinking brings only trouble, Cal."

"They drew first blood."

Doc Wilson tossed the towel to one side. "There should be law in this danged town. The railroad built it and the railroad should bring in a lawman. Those officials know this is coming up. They've worked you, Cal. The railroad has had you haul in farmers and has only backed you enough to give you a start and then break you." He stopped suddenly. For once, he had let his thoughts drive his tongue. "Now we'll leave Jimmy asleep. He'll be a sick monkey when he comes out of that chloroform." The medico opened a window. He put a blanket across the sleeping youth. Cal Rutherford looked at the pale, thin face.

Somebody knocked on the door.

Doc Wilson glanced at Jimmy, saw he was covered. "Come in."

Eddie Malone had red hair. Paul and Gertrude Malone had christened their only child Edwina some twenty-two years before, but she was known as Eddie the length and breadth of Puma Valley. The first thing you noticed was her red hair. It curled from under a cream-colored Stetson, and the lamplight danced from it in copperish waves. It was beautiful.

Then you noticed the girl herself—the thin nose, the slightly wide mouth, the green-grey eyes. This time she wore buckskin—a buckskin jacket and split buckskin riding-skirt. Her blouse was of white silk and her half-boots were bright with leather decorations.

"I just heard about Jimmy," she told Cal.

Cal said, "Oh." There was little else he could say. For a long time—ever since coming into Puma Valley—he had admired Eddie Malone. He was young—and he had a young man's dreams . . . and a young man's hopes. He had wanted to make advances. But she was the daughter of Paul Malone, and Paul Malone owned the big Heart Circle and therefore Eddie was on the other side of the fence.

Rumor had it she was friendly with Pete Glenn. Glenn was the type that attracted women—he was courteous, smiling, well-dressed, flattering. Cal Rutherford knew that Pete Glenn escorted her to the local dances. He had gone to a dance or two and seen them together.

He hadn't liked that sight.

She looked at Cal now, and the gold of her golden head showed reflections from the dim lamp. "Dad and I drove a few steers into town for the butcher," she said. "I just happened to hear about Jimmy's accident."

"He'll come through," Cal said.

"Dad had nothing to do with the accident,

23

Cal. He's been in town all afternoon. We got into town about one."

Cal nodded.

Doc Wilson was re-packing his bag. Jimmy Stephens breathed steadily and noisily. Eddie Malone scowled slightly. Cal had been rather abrupt. She knew why he had been that way. Her father had riders who could have slugged Jimmy, wrecked the grain-wagon. Paul Malone would not necessarily have to be with them when they had jumped the wagon. If the assailants had been Malone Heart Circle riders. . . .

"Dad had nothing to do with the accident, Cal."

"I'm glad to hear that."

She bit her bottom lip slightly. She was irritated and her eyes showed this. But apparently she brushed her feeling aside. How was Jimmy getting along? What were the extent of his injuries?

"Doc knows more about it than I do," Cal said.

Cal Rutherford went outside into the night with its stars. The slow wind whispered through the cottonwoods, making the leaves rustle, bending thick branches slightly. Somewhere somebody was burning trash, and the smoke

24

was a musty smell against the mystery of the night.

Cal closed his eyes.

He could see the kid, lying in there, asleep under chloroform. He could see the grain-wagon, crashed and broken, out there in the gully. He had been waiting for Jimmy to come in when the livery-barn owner had come running through the night, had come running into the elevator along the railroad tracks.

"Cal, where are you?"

"Over here, Mike."

"Cal, your teams just come in! Somebody's unhitched them an' they've kicked their double-trees loose an' they've busted lines! Only three hosses come in. The other must be dead or fouled up with his lines somewhere!"

Cal had stood wooden-faced, hiding his consternation. Then he and the hostler had hurried toward the barn. While Cal had hooked a team to a buckboard, the hostler had gone after Doc Wilson.

"Doc ain't in town, Cal. Done heard he is out treatin' that nester's sick boy an' he oughta be back soon."

"If he comes in before I get back, tell him to ride out after me."

25

"Sure thing, Cal."

Cal had laid the whip across Old Baldy. He did not spare the sorrels as he ran them through the night. Under him the buckboard jounced and bumped over the uneven road. He had met Jimmy, gone down and looked at the wreckage, and grimness had possessed him as he climbed out of the canyon and got up on the high seat of the buckboard, panting from the hard climb up the grade.

"You close to comfortable, Jimmy?"

"I'll live, Cal."

Jimmy lay on the floor of the rig. Going back, Cal did not drive as fast, for he did not want to jounce the youth too much. He questioned Jimmy about the accident. No, he hadn't identified an attacker—all wore masks. Besides, it happened too fast. Jimmy was tired and sick and Cal asked him no other questions.

Doc Wilson had met them a mile out of town and together the medico and elevator-man had carried the youth into the doctor's office. Now, standing there under the stars, Cal Rutherford remembered the pained, hurt look on the boy's thin face. It haunted him; it drove him.

But where and whom would he hit?

He had analyzed his problem down to its

essentials. He had three enemies. One was the railroad. He had moved in, built his elevator, got in farmers, and all the time he had trusted the railroad officials, thinking they would work together and therefore profit together.

That idea had proven wrong. Now he understood the railroad officials had used him as a buffer against Pete Glenn and Paul Malone. The railroad had got him to invest his money in the elevator and to move in the first farmers. Unwittingly he had been used.

Every dollar he had was tied up in this scheme. His father had run cattle down in Colorado for a few years before dying. His mother had followed his dad into death inside a year. He had sold their herds and put his money into his farming scheme. But he had been wrong to trust the railroad.

From long habit he looked up at the sky. But if there were any clouds the night hid them. The Sunday before the farmers had gathered at Willow Creek school and prayed for rain. Apparently their prayers had been useless.

His only hope—and the hope of the sodbusters—was that it would rain. Rain for at least a day. If rain came, their crops would be sure to come through with a fair yield, unless hail took the wheat later on. But when would it rain? Who was master of the elements?

He had the railroad to buck . . . and he faced two cowmen. Paul Malone and Pete Glenn. . . . Now one of them had jumped his grain-tank and destroyed it. For a moment a blind sort of rage ran riot through him. It drew color from his face and wadded his hands into hard fists.

If only Jimmy had recognized at least one attacker. . . .

But he hadn't. That angle, then, was out—it was worthless, useless. Out of this tragedy had come nothing concrete. Only the broken wagon and the teams with their harnesses kicked to pieces. He could not hit at either Pete Glenn or Paul Malone.

Eddie had said her father had had nothing to do with this dastardly attack against a sixteen-year-old boy. . . . Cal found himself hoping she was right; he wanted, for some reason, to believe her. He looked at a townsman who was coming toward him, boots ringing on the thick plank walk.

"How's Jimmy, Cal?"

"Hip was dislocated." Cal spoke shortly. "He'll be up an' around in a few days, so Doc says."

28

"That's good."

Cal was silent. The man was silent. Finally the man said, "Pete Glenn is down in the saloon, Cal. He's drinking and he's lost some money gamblin' an' he's mean. He's got Marfa Jordan with him."

"Marfa Jordan goes where Glenn goes," Cal said. "He slings a gun for Glenn. Thanks, fellow."

"That's okay, Cal."

The man moved off, evidently heading for home. Cal Rutherford listened to the dying pound of the man's justins. News travelled fast in this little burg. Quick tongues as in every small town. By this time the farmers would know about Jimmy's accident.

This townsman, he knew, had been warning him in a subtle way. For Pete Glenn would be wary toward him. Glenn was no fool; neither was Paul Malone. Both would know Cal Rutherford watched them angrily.

The elevator owner looked at the Down Ace saloon, about sixty feet down the street. While the rest of the town at this late hour was dark, there was a light in the Down Ace. Cal knew that Pete Glenn liked to gamble and he heard Glenn was a good gambler. And he had also

29

heard of Glenn's terrible temper when the cards ran against him.

Behind him, the door to Doc Wilson's office opened. He turned and looked at Eddie Malone. He expected the girl to go to the hotel, but she stopped beside him, and he noticed she looked toward the Down Ace.

"Cal, why don't you go to bed, and think this over until tomorrow? Sleep on it, Cal."

Cal jerked a thumb toward the doc's office. "I'm thinking of that kid in there. He could have got killed. Doc took three stitches in that wound in his scalp."

"Sleep on it, Cal."

Antagonism rolled through the elevator-man. Everything in the last few months had turned out wrong. This was an irritating, rubbing, galling thought. It made him say, "Are you afraid I'll hurt your friend, Pete Glenn?"

"Go to the devil." She walked away.

Cal watched her go into the hotel, heard her slam the door. He had acted like a kid, he knew; this thought was not pleasant, either. But Eddie was right. He had best give this trouble sincere consideration before making a move. He turned and started toward his bed in his office.

He was passing in front of the Down Ace when a man spoke from the darkened doorway.

"Walk on light boots, Rutherford!"

3

THE words were harsh and they stopped Cal Rutherford and they turned him. And he stood there with this anger inside of him, and he had the memory of Jimmy Stephens back there in Doc Wilson's office.

"Who talks there?"

The man came out of the doorway and said, "Marfa Jordan." He stopped and looked at Cal and he was a block of granite against the night.

Cal watched him. There was a trap here and this knowledge kept beating inside of him. Marfa Jordan slung a quick gun on Pete Glenn's payroll. Cal looked back at the darkened doorway. Nobody stood there. Marfa Jordan had been waiting for him to come along.

For a moment, fear plucked at Cal's nerves. He was not armed. Jordan always carried two guns. Then the elevator-owner realized that violence could not be carried so far, even in a town without formal law. For you cannot shoot down an unarmed man regardless of how lawless a range might be.

Still, there was a trap here. He could feel it and smell it and taste it, and he waited.

"What do you want, Jordan?"

Marfa Jordan walked with a rolling, lumbering gait. His long arms hung at his thick thighs. He reminded Cal of an ape. Jordan had power in those hands and those long arms.

"There's a rumor around you claim I helped run that grain-wagon of your'n off that canyon."

Now Cal had the full significance of this trap. Jordan was only acting on Pete Glenn's orders. For Cal had made no such statement. In fact, with the exception of Doc Wilson, he had made no mention to anybody—outside of his few words with Eddie Malone—about the accident. Now Jordan was only using this as an opening wedge for trouble.

"You heard wrong," Cal said.

Marfa Jordan stood silent, watching him. Cal could only guess at the tension in the man. But this was no time or place for trouble. Cal turned, and a long arm went out, and a heavy hand dug fingers into his shoulder. Anger ran through Cal and he smashed the hand from his shoulder.

He brought his right forearm in, blocking,

hitting. He hacked down and his forearm smashed across Marfa Jordan's wrist. Maybe Cal caught the man off-guard. Maybe Jordan wasn't expecting the sudden jarring blow.

Anyway, Cal knocked the fingers loose. They gripped again, but this time they did not get flesh but tore into Cal's shirt. The shirt ripped with a slithering sound that for some reason was loud in the night. And Marfa Jordan held cloth in his thick hand.

Cal waited no longer. He was sure that, in a rough-and-tumble fight, Jordan could whip him. He had a momentary advantage. He had Marfa Jordan off-balance, and he hit hard with both fists, working them in one after the other, and hitting hard.

Blood quick in him, he realized he had knocked Marfa Jordan back a pace or two. He heard the grunt of the gunman. It was a wheezing sound that held surprise. And it told Cal Rutherford he had shaken the ape-like gunman.

This knowledge bright, he went ahead—and he walked into a wall. A wall that swung out of the night and smashed into him. By sheer will-power he managed to hold his feet under him. Dimly he then realized he had not hit a stone wall. He had stopped Marfa Jordan's wild-swinging right fist.

Another blow like that, Cal Rutherford, and you'll go down! A voice inside, confused and dim, seemed to repeat that. He ducked, and Marfa Jordan missed his next hit and walked into Cal's fists.

It was like beating a big sandstone rock. Cal thought he would break his right wrist. One blow caught Marfa Jordan in the throat. Knuckles tore up and smashed into the man's left jaw. And Marfa Jordan went down.

He went sprawling backwards, arms working the air as if to grasp support there. He was gasping something; not words, just grunts. But there were no hand-holds in the air and Jordan landed sitting down about ten feet away. Cal heard something metallic hit the sidewalk. He caught the glimpse of steel and knew one of Jordan's pistols had slipped leather and slid from holster.

Cal stood, legs wide, fists heavy. He waited, sucking in air. He was more surprised than Jordan. He was sure of that. So far, he'd been lucky. Lucky blows, lucky to catch the gunman off-balance. He was aware that men were coming from the Down Ace Saloon. But he paid them little attention, for he concentrated his attention on Marfa Jordan.

Jordan muttered, "That was an accident. You can't do it again, Rutherford." He was talking low. He was stunned, and Cal got the impression the words were not so much for him, as they were to encourage Jordan. Jordan's pride and fighting ability had taken a hard knock-down.

As for himself, the knock-down over Jordan had given him new hope. He felt better now. In the fierce burst of fighting, he had somehow gotten rid of lots of his indecision and uncertainty. He had lost it in the red wave of physical action.

Still, he doubted if he could whip Jordan. Jordan was of such low intelligence he had great pride in his fighting ability. Marfa Jordan would fight even harder now. And Cal Rutherford had his doubts.

He saw Doc Wilson, standing with Eddie Malone. He glanced at Eddie, but if her eyes held anything, the night hid them. Pete Glenn and two riders stood to one side and Glenn watched Jordan, down there on the sidewalk.

Cal panted, "You get enough, Jordan?"

The question didn't make sense. Jordan

would fight more—he'd fight until knocked out or dead—and every man there, including Cal, knew this. Cal wanted to get out of this fight. Nothing would be accomplished. He and Jordan would just beat each other, and the original problem would sit to one side and come no nearer to a solution.

"I'm comin' up," Jordan growled.

Pete Glenn said clearly, "You better get up, you big scissor-bill! 'Cause if'n you don't, you might just as well ride past the Bar N!"

Jordan said, "T'hell with you!" and came up. Cal circled, and he heard Doc Wilson say, "Fight him from a distance, Cal. Don't move in on him. He's got too much strength an' he's got the reach."

Cal heard the words as if from a great distance. While waiting for Jordan to get up he had decided upon his plan of attack. He was no fist-fighter. He had had his share of fights and he had been taught a little science. But he was hard. A man can't shovel wheat all day without getting good leg and shoulder-muscles and getting corrugations across his belly.

Doc Wilson was only repeating the plan Cal had thought out. Jordan had the weight and the strength and the reach. Cal would have to fight him from a distance—blocking, ducking, running, circling. His only hope was to wear Jordan down.

But he had to move three feet while Marfa Jordan moved one foot. For while he circled, Marfa Jordan only had to turn. Jordan was puzzled at first. Up to now, men had carried the fight to him; he'd stood and battered them down and matched strength and fists in a sharp display.

This was a new way of fighting, Jordan saw. He drew his forehead down and pulled his head down between his thick shoulders. This elevator-man wasn't hitting hard, but still his blows were not comforting. Jordan glimpsed an opening. His right fist swung.

Cal Rutherford took the blow full on.

By this time, Rutherford's lips were cut, and the salty taste of blood was in his mouth. His head was not too clear. He had absorbed so much punishment he now seemed immune to further blows. But the right stunned him and drove him back, and Marfa Jordan came in.

"Circle him!"

That would still be Doc Wilson's words. Cal circled to his right now. If that right fist came in again he would be travelling with it and not against it. Jordan was wild with hope and he was wide open, and Cal punched him with rights and lefts. This time he felt Jordan give.

As for himself, he was almost done. The fight seemed to have lasted hours. He was aware of little outside of himself: once he heard Pete Glenn holler to Jordan, but the words were not clear. Once he had heard Eddie Malone call something, and he was aware that Paul Malone stood beside his daughter. Cal glimpsed the square shoulders against the night, and dismissed the cowman from his mind.

"Circle him, Cal! Keep away from him!"

That would be Doc Wilson again! The medico knew something about fighting, Cal decided. He kept on taking Doc Wilson's advice. Circling, shuffling, letting Marfa Jordan carry the fight. Marfa Jordan, who stood wide-legged, beaten across the wide face, with his shirt hanging from his belt in ribbons. And with surprise showing under the pain.

For Jordan had figured this would be a cinch. Call him and fight with him and knock him down and then give him the boots. That would be all there'd be to it. It wouldn't take long and it would be easy, and then he'd collect from

Pete Glenn and buy some drinks and treat the boys and brag some more.

But it hadn't turned out that way. Cal Rutherford had dumped him, Marfa Jordan, on the sidewalk—and dumped him hard. So far, Cal hadn't been down. Jordan said, "Stand still, you scissorbill, an' fight!" He shuffled ahead, and Cal saw his opening.

And Jordan's jaw was clipped shut.

Cal had waited for this opening. His second-wind was strong in him. And Doc Wilson used psychology. Doc Wilson said, "Remember that kid back there, Cal!" and the memory of Jimmy Stephens, wrapped in pain, swept across Cal Rutherford. This memory was the spur he needed. His mind was cold; his face was cold; nothing could hurt him now.

"Follow in, Cal! You got him!"

Doc Wilson again. . . . Doc, watching with objective eyes, seeing Marfa Jordan's weak spots. . . . Cal saw Jordan was on his boot-heels. That hard blow—that last clean smash—had stopped Jordan!

Cal went to work. He worked with a cold methodical deadliness. He was dogged and sure. He was in pain, but Jimmy Stephens was in pain, too. Jimmy had smiled through his pain. Cal Rutherford fought through his.

Later, when the fight was over, he wondered about himself. For he realized he had lost his head. But he had not gone into a hot fury, as so many people do when they lose their perspective; he had gone into a cold controlled fury, fury all the more deadly because of its objectiveness.

This had fired sagging, tired muscles. It had brought him ahead, right boot crossed, and it had pulled his head down, making his skull a bobbing, weaving target. It had done this and more. It had made him weave and pitch and throw out straight blows—blows that came out level with his shoulder.

Doc Wilson told him afterwards he had never seen a man fight with such cold dispatch, either in or out of the ring. But it was the thought of Jimmy Stephens that did it. Jimmy was the only human on this range of intrigue and greed who loved him. Jimmy was the only human who was really his friend.

His right found Marfa Jordan's jaw. It pulled back the man's head as if a heavy rope had jerked him. The left came in and the man went back. He was staggering, and he hit and missed, and he put his back against the Down Ace Saloon. And that left came in again and that right followed.

Jordan grunted something; a right closed his mouth. He must have known then he was done for. He brought up his forearms and tried to shield his face. But Cal's blows knocked his arms to one side. And then Cal came in.

This time, Jordan could not retreat. Cal used his head and he butted him; he smashed his head into Jordan's, and hooked his jaw over Jordan's shoulder. He beat Jordan in the belly. He got one blow and it was hard, but he let it go without notice. For he knew no pain.

He broke, and he back-slapped Jordan. He ran both fists across the man's face and felt blood. Jordan was sobbing something, and then Cal caught him. He dropped the man. Jordan slid down, back to the wall—two blows lifted him. He was out, and his head lolled back and his eyes were those of a sledge-hammered steer. And Cal stepped back and let the man drop.

And Marfa Jordan was unconscious. He sat down and then came to rest on his right side. Cal watched, fists doubled. He stood like that, and Jordan lay still, and Cal felt a hand on his shoulder.

"Don't hit me, boy."

Cal let his fists drop. He opened his hands and found that his knuckles were sore. He was aching across his shoulders. He tried to talk, and he said, "I'm sorry, Doc. I'm touchy, I reckon."

"You've got reason." Doc Wilson spoke quietly. "Now come to my office, son. I want to look you over."

Pete Glenn said, "Look at my man first, medico. Rutherford is on his feet."

Cal Rutherford turned and looked at the Bar N owner. "You oughta take what I gave him. He's only drawin' your wages. Maybe your men put my grain-wagon into that canyon!"

Cal started forward. Pete Glenn doubled his fists. The lamplight from the saloon caught the glimmer of hope in his eyes. But Doc Wilson stepped forward and held Cal. Paul Malone got on the side opposite Doc Wilson.

Malone said, "He's had enough for tonight. He's out on his boots an' he don't savvy it. He'd be nice pickin's for a fresh man like you, Glenn."

"Keep outa this, Malone."

Malone spoke almost too quietly. "I might . . . and I might not."

Pete Glenn stepped back. Tension ran out of Cal Rutherford. He was glad now that Doc Wilson and Paul Malone had stepped in. He was sick, dog-tired, and Glenn would have beaten him down easily.

He started to say, "Thanks, men." Then everything went black.

4

THE pinto tossed his head as he fought a stubborn nose-fly. He was a four-year-old and had been under the saddle for only a year. He had been running with a wild bunch over on Hog Ridge, and Eddie Malone had seen him one day on the rimrock. She had said, "I'm going to run that pinto down, Dad."

"You'll never do it," Paul Malone had said. "I've had a dozen men trying to gather that bunch of wild hosses. They're tricky, and so far we've run down five head. How much you got in your sock?"

"A pretty leg."

"I know that, chicken. But I'm not talkin' about the sock you got on. I mean the one you keep the paper money in."

"Fifty bucks."

"I'll lay one-fifty against your fifty you won't dab twine on that pinto."

"You're called, sucker."

Within three months Eddie was cutting out cattle on the pinto. She never told her dad how she had caught him. Actually she had caught him in a horse-trap she herself had designed. And old Paul Malone grinned when he paid her.

"You'll get any man you set after, chicken."

"I reckon I will."

She had worked cattle and horses ever since the day she had been able to sit on her chubby pony. Paul and Gertrude Malone had sent her out winters for school and she had got through high-school. Gertrude was bound to make her what she called a "lady," and despite Eddie's protests had enrolled her in a girl's college. Eddie had lasted three weeks before they had kicked her out.

"Dad, I'll tell you this, and I won't tell Mom. But I slapped that dean on purpose so I would get the boot."

"All right with me, chicken."

"If I ever see another book it's only going to be a cook-book."

"You'd need one," Paul Malone had said.

Now the pinto lept fighting the bit. And Eddie said, "Always something wrong with a bronc—if it ain't mosquitoes, it's horse-flies."

"They're like humans that way."

The girl looked at her father, who rode a big

grey gelding. Paul Malone and the saddle were one. He never tanned. He only got redder.

"What'd you mean, dad?"

Paul Malone groaned in sham disgust. "My Gawd, girl, do I have to draw a blueprint? Sometimes I reckon you're as dumb as your mother. Us humans here in Puma Valley are weighted down with troubles, and they ain't horse-flies, either. Some of them'll sound mebbe like hoss-flies with a big buzz—but they'll be bullets singing!"

"Maybe it won't get that far."

"You sound optimistic. In fact, you sound downright hopeful." Malone turned in saddle, hand braced on his cantle. "You seen Cal Rutherford batter down that human ape of a Marfa Jordan. You seen Pete Glenn's eyes, didn't you?"

"I'm not in the habit of looking into Glenn's eyes."

Paul Malone turned back in leather. He let his grey plod along. He laced his big knuckled hands over the saddle-horn. He might have been talking to himself. He was very sincere.

"Pete Glenn's bossed the south side of Puma Valley for a long, long time. When he figured he couldn't whip a man, he's always sicked

Marfa Jordan on him. They claim Marfa Jordan came from Texas, an' somewhere on the trail north he decided to change his name for personal reasons. So he took the name of Marfa County for a headname and the land beyond the Pearly Gates for the back-name."

"He'll never see the Pearly Gates."

"That ain't for us to debate about, chicken. The point is that Marfa Jordan won't rest until either he or Cal Rutherford is dead."

"Are you sure of that?"

Something in his daughter's voice caused Paul Malone to send her a quick searching glance.

"Sure, I'm sure of that. Jordan has a rep as a gunslinger. He's iggnerant, an' he likes that rep—the next time he calls Rutherford it'll be with cutters. An' what kind of a han' is this elevator-man with a pistol?"

"He's a good shot."

"How do you know?"

"Cal and Jimmy and I were out behind the elevator one day. We were practicing with Cal's .45. He had it holstered, and a rabbit jumped out about twenty yards away, and the first thing I knew that rabbit was rolling and a shot was roaring in my ears. He's quick with a gun."

"You seem to know a lot about that scissor-bill, huh?"

"He's no scissor-bill!"

Paul Malone's red Irish face showed a small smile. He was an expert at deviling his daughter and wife. He had been sure for some time that Edwina was interested in Cal Rutherford. This had bothered him, but he had never said anything about it: he and Rutherford were on opposite sides of a high, high fence.

"Maybe it'd be best if Jordan did kill Rutherford."

Eddie turned on him, the sunlight flashing off her red hair. "You talk like a complete sap sometimes, Dad. Rutherford is a man, while that Jordan is just a low-down killer hired by Pete Glenn. I've asked Glenn why he kept such a terrible man on his payroll."

"What answer'd he give you?"

"None that was satisfactory."

Malone regarded the horizon again. "He wouldn't. Pete Glenn is slippery. He's like a carp you just caught in a swamp. He'll slide right outa your hands if you ain't careful."

Eddie took the simile wrong. "He won't slide out of my hands, Dad. He's all right, I guess, but he's not for me."

"That's the trouble with you heifers!" Paul Malone exploded. "You take a man too literal all the time! I was just makin' a comparison!"

Eddie's eyes danced. "Oh . . . I'm sorry."

"You're not sorry an' you know it! But who in blazes jumped this kid Jimmy an' slugged him an' run his wagon off the grade?"

Eddie spoke very carefully. "Sure you didn't have some Heart Circle riders out last night?"

Again Paul Malone regarded his daughter. But this time his eyes were cold and his red jowls redder than ever.

"Eddie, do you really mean that?"

"I don't know, Dad. Maybe I do; maybe I don't. But it simmers down to one thing, whether you like it or not: either you or Pete Glenn had men to run off with that wagon and wreck it."

Paul Malone was silent. The cowman was no fool. He had as much brains as God handed out to the ordinary man. He used his brains now. Eddie was right, much as he hated to admit it. Either his men or Bar N men had dumped that wagon down that grade and slugged Jimmy Stephens.

People would look at it that way. Cal Rutherford would view it in that manner.

There was war ahead. Grim, bitter war that could end in quite a few deaths. There had been other scattered nester-cowmen wars across the West. Just recently Wyoming had had a vicious outbreak of wars pitching farmers against cowmen. Nate Champion had recently died, shot through and through, in a burning cabin down in Johnson county below the Wyoming-Montana border.

The militia had come into Johnson County and restored a semblance of order. But still, Nate Champion was dead. . . . Paul Malone didn't like it one bit the way things were shaping up on Puma Valley grass. And he didn't want a Puma Valley war.

At first he had been violently against the farmers, advocating violence to keep them out. Then he had given it serious thought. Slowly his opinion had changed. He was still against the farmers. But now he would not fight them.

For he realized such a fight would be useless. He could never win. The days of open government-range were over with. They had run their cycle and now that cycle had ended.

He had told this one day to Pete Glenn.

"I don't agree with you, Paul," Glenn had shaken his head. "Them sodbusters ain't got no

51

guts. Let one of them get in a shootin' fray an' get killed, an' the others'll pull out pronto. That's my theory."

"Don't figger you're right, Pete."

"No way to tell but to do as I said," Pete Glenn said. "Maybeso some of these days I'll notch me off the hide of a nester. Or do you reckon to beat me to it, Malone?"

"Don't reckon so, Pete."

Glenn had given Paul Malone a long steady look. Down the bar, Marfa Jordan had looked at Malone, and Marfa Jordan's animal-like eyes had been hidden behind deceptive eyelids.

"You backin' out on us, Paul?"

Paul Malone had spoken quietly. "What you do, Pete, is your business, not mine. I've looked over a few hands of poker in my life. I don't tip my hand. You can take your answer outa that, fella."

Paul Malone had walked out.

Pete Glenn had looked at Marfa Jordan and winked. Malone had not seen this wink. Now Malone wondered just where Pete Glenn and Jordan stood in this warfare. He was sure the Bar N riders had dumped Cal Rutherford's grain-tank off the canyon. He had given his

Heart Circle men orders not to pick trouble with the farmers or Cal Rutherford.

But some of his hands were pretty bitter against the farmers. They had punched Heart Circle cattle for years. Malone had tried to point out to them that, even if more farmers came, the Heart Circle would not go out of business. They'd run cattle back in the timber and buy hay from the sodmen for winter feeding.

"It'll mean we cut the amount of cattle we run, Eddie. But we can get in some good bulls and make our cows throw better calves. A cowman's memory is short. But me, I can't forget the winter of '86 an' '87."

That winter hundreds of native steers and cows had frozen to death. Some big outfits lost over fifty per cent of their herds. Cattle drifted against drift-fences and a cowboy could walk over the fence on their frozen carcasses. Cattle died for the simple reason that the cowmen had overstocked ranges. And another reason was that cowmen had neglected to put up hay for winter feeding.

Glenn was one of those cowmen who ran cattle out on range in the winter-time and did not put up hay. But Paul Malone had learned his lesson. When spring had come in 1887 he had ridden out across a range that was dotted with the bloated carcasses of Heart Circle cattle. Each summer he cut native hay and stacked it for winter feeding. Now this year he aimed to buy feed off some of the farmers.

"Unless it rains, chicken, them farmers'll have to cut their wheat an' oats for feed, an' I'll buy a thousan' or so ton. Make good winter-feed. I reckon you'll see the Heart Circle in Puma Valley for a long, long time yet."

"Hope you're right, Dad."

They rode into the Heart Circle yard. This was a big, sprawling ranch, strung along the bottom of a creek, the stream running through the middle of the big barn. An old man came out of the barn and said, "I'll take your broncs."

"I'm not too old to unsaddle my own cayuse, Ike."

Old Ike took the reins from Malone anyway. Eddie went to the house, but her father went over and talked with two cowboys looking at some broomtails in the corral. He told them about Jimmy Stephens' so-called accident. He watched them carefully. There was nothing but surprise on their faces.

"All the men stay in camp last night?" Malone asked.

"Reckon we all was here, wasn't we, Smoky?"

Smoky nodded. "All in camp."

5

PETE GLENN and Marfa Jordan left Puma City within the hour after Cal Rutherford had whipped the big Bar N gunhand. Jordan had washed his face in the horse trough down by the livery stable. He had splashed water and blown like a whale, and Pete Glenn had stood and watched him and had been silent.

This silence bothered Marfa Jordan. He didn't like the way Pete Glenn looked at him, either. Jordan's face was cut on the left cheek and the eyebrow on his right eye was ripped loose by Cal Rutherford's fists. His upper lip was getting as thick as the leather on a saddle-skirt.

"You don't like my looks, Pete?"

Pete Glenn smiled coldly. "You won't win no beauty contest, even among a bunch of milk cows. You figure you oughta get some stitches in that eyebrow."

"It'll grow back together."

Glenn shrugged. "Your trouble, fella. Now let's get our cayuses an' hit outa town, huh?"

They had untied broncs, found stirrups, and gone up. Glenn had moved quickly into saddle, but Marfa Jordan had grunted as he had risen. Glenn led the way, putting his bronc to a lope, and Pete Glenn was light in stirrups. But Marfa Jordan rode deep between rim and horn and had boots deep in his ox-bow stirrups.

They loped out of town and the buildings fell behind. They swung south, following a well-travelled road—the road to the Bar N. Glenn's bronc got lathered across the shoulders, the white foam forming under the silver-studded martingale, and finally the Bar N man drew the horse in, pulling him down to a running-walk. Now Marfa Jordan rode abreast his boss.

Jordan said, "Say something, Pete."

This time Pete Glenn smiled. Jordan was a little boy, whipped for the first time, and he wanted sympathy. But the Bar N owner's smile was short-lived.

"You met your match, fella, an' he trimmed you."

This drew a frown to Marfa Jordan. He touched his thick upper lip. "He got me on the jump from the start. He got in first blow an' I

57

never did get right in my boots from then on. But the next time my fists take first tally."

"You won't fight him again . . . not with fists, anyway."

Marfa Jordan looked at Pete Glenn. "Not with fists, huh? With a gun, eh?" He put his head back and he laughed silently. "My gun can do it, too. She's never laid down on me."

"You said that about your fists . . . until today."

Pete Glenn was joshing Marfa Jordan, but under it all there was a serious vein. Jordan knew that the cowman was angry with him. But the gun-hand liked this Puma Valley range and he liked the wages Pete Glenn paid him.

"I'll gun down Cal Rutherford the next time I see him."

"You match guns with him when I say the word—and not before."

Marfa Jordan looked inquiringly at his boss.

Pete Glenn waved an arm out over Puma Valley. "See those farm-shacks out yonder? Each one of them houses a nester who's faithful to Cal Rutherford. You kill Rutherford, an' them nesters might organize an' get guns."

"They might run, too."

Glenn shook his head. "They might run . . .

an' they might fight. The best thing, Jordan, is to play our cards close. Rutherford's got big odds against him. He's deep in debt to the railroad. His farmers are grumblin'—they're broke an' there's no rain.

"Rutherford don't know about me an' Paul Malone. He figgers we're his enemies but he's not just sure where either of us stand. Right now he's tryin' to figure out who dumped that grain-wagon off'n the grade an' who slugged that Stephens kid. He don't know whether it's me who did it or if Paul Malone engineered it."

"Our boys worked that slick," Jordan grumbled.

They were in the southern foothills. Pete Glenn braced his right hand on the cantle of his saddle and turned halfway on stirrups to look back over Puma Valley. Somberness came into his eyes. Marfa Jordan watched him. He saw the play of greed and desire, hate and ambition, and this lighted the blocky face set on that thick neck. Lighted it and showed the man's purpose.

"What about Paul Malone?" Jordan asked.

Pete Glenn came back to earth. He swung in saddle and looked at Jordan. Then he said, "Malone is undecided. We know one thing for certain: Malone don't love one Pete Glenn.

We've been in this valley for a long time an' we've been at sword points. I never squired Eddie Malone to these dances for nothin'. She figured if she went with me it would kinda smooth things over between the Bar N and the Heart Circle. She never knew I took her to question her."

Jordan listened, beaten head cocked.

"The Bar N has no friends, Jordan. When this is over we'll control Puma Valley. We'll take over Cal Rutherford's interests. With luck, we should boss the Heart Circle."

"Big job, Pete."

"Time'll tell."

They were silent after that. Pete Glenn had his plans, his hopes; Marfa Jordan found much here he did not understand. Jordan decided he would let Glenn do the brain-work while he would insure his share through his gun and his fists. But he hadn't done so well down in Puma City against Cal Rutherford.

Because of his low intelligence, this thought ground against him with the cutting edge of coarse sandpaper. He had lost face in that fist fight. He was still convinced Cal Rutherford had not beaten him squarely. Rutherford had hit first and gained the sudden advantage.

Rutherford had then doggedly followed up and capitalized on this advantage.

The next time they fought . . . well, it would be different. He would jump Rutherford first and ask questions afterwards. Or maybe he wouldn't give the elevator-man a chance. There'd be the darkness and an alley and a man coming out of that darkness. . . .

That would be best, he decided.

Then his decision became reversed. If he jumped Cal Rutherford and waylaid him and beat him up without any spectators, he would not regain his old lost fighting prestige. No eyes would be there to see him redeem himself. No, it would be in the open, then.

This decision made, he would wait for a chance to carry it out. So he asked, "Where we headin' for, Pete?"

"Lime Crick line-camp."

An hour later they slid broncs down a talus cone and came in on Lime Creek. This stream was composed of pot-holes, most of them dry because of the drought, and over yonder a mile or so a devil-twist of wind spiralled, lifting the white alkali dust that had given this section its name.

This dust came in and caught with the sweat

on their broncs and gave them a whitish color. The white alkali rose and coated their legs and the smart of it was in their nostrils. Here grew spiny greasewood, for no sagebrush or blue joint grass would grow here. The sparse grass was salt-grass—wiry and without taste to cattle who would not graze on it.

Against the northern rim of the flat was a grove of small, stunted cottonwood trees. Pete Glenn had had some of these cut down and had made a small cabin where he kept a man during the rainy season and in the spring when water ran off the hills and Lime Creek's chuck-holes were filled with water. This puncher would ride bog holes to see no Bar N cows got bogged. When the rain subsided and the pot-holes lost their water, the cow-puncher left the cottonwood line-camp.

Therefore the line-camp was deserted during summer, fall, and winter. But when Marfa Jordan and Pete Glenn rode up, a man came out of the buckbrush. He was a short man, dressed in a blue suit, the legs crammed into half-boots. He had a wide, intelligent face, a close-cropped moustache, and a cream-colored Stetson sat pushed back to show tawny hair.

"Figured you gents would head this way

soon." The man looked at Marfa Jordan. "Did our half-wit friend here stick his head into the rollers on Cal Rutherford's lift in the elevator?"

"Don't saddle me," Marfa Jordan growled.

A hardness entered the man's eyes and Pete Glenn caught his gaze and the cowman shrugged. The man shrugged and put his rifle against a tree and crouched, building a cigarette. Glenn came down and settled beside him, and the man handed the Bar N owner the makings.

"Well, Glenn?"

Pete Glenn licked his cigarette. "You an' the boys did all right, Hutchinson. Cal Rutherford found his wagon this mornin'. The kid was hurt an' is in bed now with a dislocated hip."

"Stephens recognize any of us?"

"Not a one of you. His light went out too fast when you boys slugged him. The wagon is wrecked, I understand."

"That'll scare these nesters," Hutchinson said. He got to his feet and spat out his smoke. The cigarette lay on the alkali and smoked, and the man seemed to be interested in the cigarette. But Pete Glenn, watching him, knew this was just a pose to hide Hutchinson's real thoughts.

"That sure should scare those farmers," Hutchinson repeated.

Glenn switched his smoke to the opposite corner of his mouth. Finally he said, "It might be the right time, Hutchinson."

Hutchinson nodded. "I'll sound out a few farmers. I'll try to buy them out. And I won't pay them too much." He showed a wry smile. "I'll see you down in town some day soon, Pete."

"Okay, fella."

Glenn and Jordan rode out, and once Glenn looked back. Somewhere in that grove stood Hutchinson, but Glenn could not see him. They swung out toward the Bar N this time, and Marfa Jordan put his bronc close.

"You trust this Hutchinson?"

Glenn shook his head. "I trust nobody, Marfa. Sometimes I doubt if I trust myself."

"He's a city man," Jordan said.

Pete Glenn held back his smile. Jordan was like the rest of the working-men. Get a new suit on a man, see that he had no calluses on his hands, and instantly men start to distrust him because he works by his brains and not by sweat.

Glenn said, "He's a big mogul with the railroad. He's playin' a game similar to ours. You get water in on Puma Valley and it'll bloom like the proverbial rose. Hutchinson aims to control that land. Then, when he controls it, he can talk turkey to the railroad officials, because he's one of them."

"What if the rest of the officials get wise to Hutchinson?"

Glenn shrugged. "How can they get wise? Hutchinson is division-superintendent of this division. If he wants more farmers in, he can let them in; if he doesn't want any, none come in. But he wants that bottom-land, and he'll get it at his own price if this drought keeps up."

"He'll break Cal Rutherford, too?"

Glenn looked at his gunman. "You know an' I know Cal Rutherford came into this country with a few thousand bucks. He's got it all tied up in his elevator and his farming land. An elevator has to turn over wheat into box-cars to make a profit. So far, Rutherford hasn't got much wheat. If this drought continues he won't get any, either."

"He's talking irrigation, Pete."

"But it takes dinero to dig ditches and build dams—and Rutherford hasn't got that money. Neither have these farmers. And with

Hutchinson bossin' Rutherford, Rutherford ain't gettin' no money from the railroad, either. When this is over, Hutchinson'll own Rutherford's land an' his elevator."

"Where do you stand, Pete?"

"What'd you mean?"

Jordan shrugged. "So far it's all Hutchinson this, Hutchinson that. . . . Where does Pete Glenn stand?"

Glenn's smile was thin. "You can think . . . at that. . . . Marfa, when this is over, Hutchinson an' me'll come out openly as partners. Back in my safe at the ranch is a signed agreement—signed by me an' Hutchinson."

"Yeah. . . ."

"When this is over Hutchinson an' me'll own Puma Valley. An' own it with deeds to every inch of land. Deeds Hutchinson has bought for a few cents on the dollar from the farmers. Where will that put Paul Malone?"

Marfa Jordan laced his thick fingers around his saddle-horn. He was catching the light now, but it was still dim.

"Malone can't run cattle on the basin. You two'll own all the land. Malone will have to run back in the hills.

"We'll control all the hay land. Malone's got

66

some puncher staked out on some grass, but that won't be much. And when winter comes an' Malone is short of feed we sell him hay at a big price. A price so big he can't hope to pay. And when the last chip is down we'll rod the Heart Circle outfit."

"Wonder if Malone is suspicious?"

"I don't figger so."

They rode toward the Bar N, with Marfa Jordan trying to think this thing through, and with Pete Glenn holding the significance of it bright in his mind. Glenn knew that if settlers stayed his days as a big cowman were numbered. He had happened to mention this one day when Hutchinson had been standing on the depot in Puma City. The railroad official had given him a long, slow look.

"I figure you got some brains, Pete Glenn. Come into the office, fellow; we've got a long talk together."

Both were greedy. An empire was at stake, ready to be had by scheming. Now, riding into the Bar N, Pete Glenn found hunger and greed and desire stirring in him.

First, the farmers would have to become afraid. The dumping of the grain-tank down the grade would put the fear of God in them. If more hauled wheat, other grain-wagons would go down grades.

Cal Rutherford would have to be broken. Maybe it would be best if he let Marfa Jordan work that out . . . with a bullet from the brush. Or a bullet from the dark. Rutherford had to go. Rutherford was dangerous. He was the cement that held the farmers together. Break him—kill him—run him out—then the real fear would hold the sodmen.

The Bar N buildings sat against a towering hill. The buildings were like their owner—neat, clean, well-ordered. The log house had a fresh coat of white paint. The bunkhouse had a long porch and was freshly painted. The big barn was in tip-top shape.

Pete Glenn looked at his ranch, felt pride in it, and then greed came in again, telling him many things.

6

THE four-horse team laid against collars as the work-horses pulled. The chains grew taut and one slipped at its tie, the work-horses slipping ahead a little at the sudden release of pressure.

"Dig into that collar, Dewey! Chubby, get down an' dig holes! Flip, work hard, you flea-bitten son!"

The farmer made his lash sing. The horses got down and pulled harder. The load started up; then the chains held again.

"Wait a minute, Mike."

"Whoa, boys."

The horses let slack creep into tugs. The farmer laid down his reins and walked to the edge of the cut, one foot on the chain. "What's the matter, Cal?"

The sun was hot enough up on the grade, but down in the canyon the heat was unbearable. Cal Rutherford wiped his forehead again and tried to spit.

"Wagon got hung up on this boulder, Mike.

69

Give me a little slack an' I'll try to work it around."

"Need any help?"

"I can handle it, I hope. Hard climb up an' down this cut so stay where you are. What you grinnin' at, you tame ape?"

"Your mug, Cal. You look like you had a run-a-way with a team hooked to a harrow an' you fell under the harrow."

Cal smiled. "You touched me on a sore spot, Mike." He braced and got a front wheel and slid the wagon to one side. They had wired the tongue and had bolted the broken reach back together. The wheat lay in the coulee, slung out into piles, and already pack-rats and ground-squirrels had taken some of it to their dens.

Cal had decided against making any effort to salvage any of the wheat. For one thing, he couldn't get it out of the canyon except maybe in tubs with farmers handing tubs from hand to hand up the incline. That would be expensive wheat. Then, too, it would have lots of dirt in it and would have to be fanned clean and that would run the bill up still higher.

Mike Hastings had been right: his face wasn't too pretty and it felt just as bad as it looked. He had taken lots of punishment from Marfa

Jordan. One eye was black, swollen almost shut; the other was not too wide open, either. The left side of his face felt and looked as if a horse had kicked him.

He got the wheel clear, then told Mike to go ahead. The team got down and dug again and the chain tightened. This time they got the wagon up another ten feet before the chain fouled itself around a big boulder. Before letting the team slack, Cal blocked the wheels with boulders.

"Now, let some slack come, Mike."

"Okay, Cal."

Cal scrambled up the slope, cleared the chain, then slid back to where the wagon was wedged against the rocks. Another hot day. Another day with the sun in a cloudless sky and with the sun burning wheat and oats and barley. He put his hand on a rock and had to jerk it back. The rock was hot, too.

Mike Hastings was cursing. Cal could not see him because of the edge of the road. Mike cursed Pete Glenn and Paul Malone. He cursed the heat. Cal waited, grinning a little. Mike was hot-headed but his anger passed quickly. Finally the curses stopped.

"You ready, Mike."

"Your damn' right, Cal."

The chain tightened again, the wagon left its blocks. The strain against gravity was terrible. Once the tongue popped with a sharp sound that sent fear through Cal. If the tongue gave they might lose the load. He got blocks under the wheels and called for Mike to stop.

The chain slackened and Mike looked down on him. "What's wrong?"

"We'd best get some slack in that chain an' make fast to the front axle. 'Cause if that tongue breaks we lose all we've worked hard to get."

"I'll get you some slack."

With the chain loose, Cal made fast around the front axle, too. This way the shaky tongue could break and they would still hold their load. The chain tightened again. Slowly the wagon rose. It creaked and protested and almost mired down in the loose talus, but then the front wheels finally came over the cliff edge to find the hard-packed road.

The welcome sight of the front-wheel on the road brought a wild yell to Mike Hastings. The horses pulled harder and the wagon then stood on the road. Cal mopped his forehead.

"Gettin' purty hot, Mike."

Mike Hastings cursed the heat.

Cal smiled slightly. "No use cursing the sun, Mike. It can't hear you. If it could, it wouldn't do anything."

"A man's gotta cuss somethin', Cal."

"Bet plenty of farmers are cursing me," Cal said quietly. "I got them to come out here. I figured that by this time we'd have dams built and would be gettin' irrigation water. Yes, I'll bet plenty of them are swearing at me."

Mike grunted something. Cal had sort of hoped the young farmer would have said the farmers blamed their predicament upon the weather, and not upon him. He didn't like the idea of being hated.

"How was Jimmy this mornin'?" Mike asked.

Cal told him that Jimmy was getting better. He'd eaten a big breakfast and Doc Wilson said he'd be out of bed soon, although he'd have to use crutches for a while. Mike Hastings looked down into the canyon and shivered despite the heat.

"Miracle that kid lived through, Cal. Man, I wish I knowed for sure who jumped him. But it points to only two parties—Paul Malone's riders an' them cowboys of Pete Glenn. Me, I'd be more apt to say Pete Glenn, off-hand."

"Why Glenn?"

Mike drank from the canteen. "I don't figure ol' Paul Malone is too bad. One day I put the question right up to him about us farmers."

"What did he say?"

Mike grinned. "Not much, Cal. Grumbled some, but said nothin' of any value. The ol' boy seemed kinda surprised, in fact. But I still don't figure he's too bad, an' don't ask me why I figure thataway."

"I'm getting so I don't trust anybody," Cal said. "Sometimes I don't even trust myself. An' when a man gets that boogery he's in bad shape."

Mike unhooked two horses and hooked the remaining two to the grain-tank. Then he hooked his team to his wagon which stood against the cut. He inspected the grain-tank carefully.

"Reckon if it could stand the pull up that hill, Cal, it can stand the trip into town. But I wouldn't trot a team on it."

"Thanks a lot, Mike."

"That's okay."

Mike sat on his wagon-seat and watched Cal get the grain-wagon rolling. The hind wheels didn't track right, but Cal decided he could get the rig into town if he took his time. The pull had taken the ginger from his team and the broncs were content to plod now, which was all right with the elevator owner.

The hard job of getting the wagon out of the canyon had taken the stiffness out of his muscles. On awakening that morning, he had been very stiff from his fight with Marfa Jordan. The heat, coupled with sweating, had sprung the stiffness from him. He sat on the high seat and had his thoughts.

He had paid good, hard-earned money for this wagon. Now it would take the town blacksmith at least two days to bring it back into good shape. He had questioned Jimmy Stephens again, but Jimmy had not been able to identify an assailant. And a man can't act only on suspicion.

He was a few miles out of town when a rider came up on a chestnut sorrel. "Howdy, Cal."

"How are you, Hutchinson?"

"Hot." The railroad man looked at the cloudless sky. "When'll it ever rain? This is tough on these nesters, Cal."

"It ain't easy," Cal admitted slowly.

"I got in town last night," Hutchinson said. "Shipped a saddle-horse along so I could do some riding. Crops don't look too good. One or two nesters mentioned like he might sell out."

Cal nodded.

"Here's a chance to make some money," Hutchinson went on. "Buy those nesters up for a few bucks, Cal. We'll get a government irrigation project in here come a few years. Then this land will be worth money."

Cal Rutherford showed a tight smile. "Buy them up—with what, Hutchinson? You know I'm darned near broke."

Hutchinson said, "I'll see you in town," and loped ahead. Cal watched the railroad man disappear into the heat and the distance. He had never really understood Hutchinson, he realized.

For one thing, Hutchinson didn't talk too much. He made no outright promises. Cal blamed that on the railroad policy. Hutchinson was only a cog in the railroad machinery. Perhaps, had he talked too much, had he made too many promises, they might have boomeranged . . . and cost Hutchinson his soft job.

Hutchinson was a queer fellow to hold a railroad job. He'd ship in a bronc, saddle him, then head out on the range. Sometimes he'd be gone for days while talking to farmers and sizing up the situation in Puma Valley. He seemed to take a real interest in this farming scheme.

He had turned everything over to Cal. Cal had advertised, got in the farmers, and Cal had put all his money into this venture. Many times he wished he had played it smart and borrowed money from the railroad company instead of risking his own capital.

But it was too late now. He was in this to the chin and he was sinking each day. Rain would save them all. But when would rain come?

Again, Cal looked at the cloudless sky.

His team had rested, but because of the condition of his wagon he had to make slow time. He met a rig a mile out of Puma City. The blocky, red-faced farmer wiped sweat from his sun-tanned face.

"Tough luck about that wheat goin' over the ridge, Cal."

Cal nodded. "What do the rest of the farmers say, Jack Jones?"

Jones scowled. "T'tell you the truth, Cal, most of 'em are scared stiff. The women-folks are causin' most of the trouble. Some of 'em are eggin' their men real hard to get them to jerk stakes."

"Sorry to hear that, Jones."

Jones spat. "Me, I don't cotton much to this trouble. Us nesters could move against them two big cow outfits, sure—an' some of us'd get shot into hame-straps. Most of us got women an' young 'uns."

"Don't spread that talk," Cal warned.

"Me, I ain't spreadin' it, Cal. But it's runnin' aroun' from farm to farm. We don't cotton to trouble—that is, most of us don't. But if they run trouble out at us . . . well, that's a hoss of a different color."

Cal said, "Hutchinson is in town. I'll hit him up again for a loan from the railroad. Some of the farmers got a little wheat they can sell, haven't they?"

"Not much, Cal."

Cal said, "If it doesn't rain inside a week, we'd best all cut our crops for hay. Paul Malone told me he'd buy all the hay we could sell him."

"Sure, at his price."

"Might beat no money, when winter comes."

Jack Jones said, "Cal, I figger they got us whipped. When the railroad cut off our credit they done whipped us just as much as the drought. Well, giddap, ol' plugs. So long, Cal."

"So long."

7

WHEN Cal Rutherford drove the grain-wagon over to his elevator, Jimmy Stephens sat on the step of his office. He hobbled over to the wagon, walking on crutches.

"Doc says you could get outa bed, Jimmy?"

Jimmy nodded. "My hip hurts some, but that's only logical, Doc said." He looked the wagon over carefully. "You got it out in purty good shape at that, Cal. I figured it would be wrecked more than it is."

Cal unhooked his team.

"What about the wheat?" Jimmy wanted to know.

"We can't get the wheat out of there. We'd have to pass it out in buckets, and that would take a long time, and besides, it's full of dirt and then we'd have to fan it. Wouldn't be worth it, Jimmy."

"I'd like to know somethin' for sure, Cal."

Cal gave the kid a quick look. He knew what Jimmy was driving at. Jimmy wouldn't rest until he had found out who had slugged him and put the grain-tank over the cliff. And Cal didn't like that idea.

"You just forget that idea, fella." Cal Rutherford made his voice stern. "That's for me to find out. You're just working for wages for me, an' that doesn't mean you get a sudden mind to sling a gun."

Jimmy grinned. "Okay, boss." He balanced himself on his crutches. "Me an' these wooden pins get along purty good. Keep smilin', young un, an' I'll go down an' get the smithy to come up an' give this rig the once-over."

"Do that."

Jimmy stopped. "You know that purty red-headed girl, Cal? You know the one I mean— Eddie Malone?"

"Yeah."

"I believe she's done got her cap set for you."

"I hope so."

Jimmy smiled. "Heck, a man can't even rib you no longer." He hobbled off, and Cal went into his office.

Blistering heat assailed him the moment he opened the door. He pried up the windows, catching the musty odor of wheat and dust that always accumulates around a grain-elevator. He

80

went into the weighing-room. Here the planks were silvery from the shod hoofs of horses as they pulled their heavy loads upon the scales. A mouse ran into a wheat-bin.

Cal made a mental note to procure another cat as he stood and looked at the elevator in which he had put almost every cent he owned. He liked this business. He liked the smell of wheat, musty and thick. He liked the feel of oats as it slid through his fingers as the lift raised the wagons to dump the loads out the end-gates. This was the only job he had ever liked.

For one thing, this job was immense. It had no limits. There was a vision and he fitted into it. Some day wheat-tank after wheat-tank would come down the lanes of Puma Valley, horses braced against collars as they pulled in the heavy loads of wheat. With water, this basin would be a green garden.

He had given up the theory of dry-land farming. This basin just didn't get enough rain. Irrigation would be the thing. But how could he keep his farmers together until water flowed in ditches?

That was the problem.

He heard boots back in his office, and a voice called, "Hey, Cal. Where are you?"

"Coming."

Jack Hutchinson sat on a chair. He had his shirt open, showing a hairy, thick chest. "Saw Jimmy down at the smithy's. Kid said you wanted to see me. First, tell me about Jimmy's accident."

"No accident," Cal told him.

Hutchinson studied his polished boots. "Sign points to the cowmen," he said at length. "Couldn't point any other place but toward Pete Glenn and Paul Malone. It's simple. Neither wants farmers in Puma Valley."

Cal nodded.

"Which one do you think did it?"

Cal played his cards close. "I don't know."

Hutchinson crossed his legs, careful not to spoil the crease in his trousers. "I'd say Malone. He's cut fences an' run his cattle in on nester ground. I wish we had concrete evidence and we'd get a warrant for him."

"But we ain't got it."

Hutchinson stood up. "Cal, play your cards close. Watch and get some evidence. Then notify me, and the railroad will line up behind you."

Cal showed a thin smile. This sounded unlikely and he judged it a lot of wind. "So far the railroad hasn't backed me enough," he pointed out. "We need money. When I moved these farmers in here the railroad promised me money to tide them over if I ran short or if any particular farmer ran out of cash."

"They promised you up to a certain sum, Cal. That sum has been reached."

"They made that point flexible," Cal again reminded him. "The promise was to try to stay within specified limits. This drought upset us."

Hutchinson spread his hands. "I can't help it, Cal. I only work for a livin'. My job, that's all. I only do what the directors say. And in this case they say no more dinero."

"Not a cent?"

"Not a red cent."

Cal felt anger break over him. He tried to hold it but he couldn't. He had to say it. "I hear tell you've talked about buyin' out a couple of the sodmen? That true, Hutchinson?"

Hutchinson nodded, watching him.

"Whose money you usin'? The railroad's?"

Hutchinson shook his head. "My money, Cal."

Cal Rutherford shoved back his anger with

great effort. He had the feeling he was going to break. This had ridden him for days and for nights that had turned into weeks and then into months. He decided the feeling was one of futility and not one of failure. He was bucking the elements; he was bucking his fellow-man. And there seemed no loophole, no weak place, to hit.

Jack Hutchinson's thick face was sombre. Evidently he read Cal Rutherford's indecision. They had never been close friends. Only business had kept them around each other.

"I see a bargain, Cal. This land'll be worth money when water comes on it. If these home-sick sodbusters want to sell deeds at the right price I'll buy them. I'll hold the land idle until water comes in."

"That'll take quite a bit of money."

"I've got a little. I've worked years and I've made a little on investments." Hutchinson's voice was soft and confidential. "The railroad won't put in another nickel. I've even gone before the board of directors in Chicago and begged them for money for Puma Valley. But it's no use. Why don't you take a trip back east to Chicago and appeal to the directors?"

Cal grinned at that. "If they won't take your

advice, they sure won't take mine. And if I bought a ticket to Chicago, I'd never have money enough to come back, and it's a long, long walk."

"I'll do my best," Hutchinson reminded him.

Cal said, "Sorry I talked a little too much, Jack."

"I can see your predicament, Cal. I'm sorry for you. You invested money and stand to lose it if it doesn't rain."

"Rain'll have to come soon . . . or it'll be too late."

He and Hutchinson went down-town together. There was nothing to do at the elevator. Most of the farmers had sold what little grain they had got from last year's crop. Occasionally one of them hauled in a few sacks of wheat.

"A beer?" Hutchinson asked.

They went into the Down Ace. The swamper had sprinkled the floor with water and therefore it was a little cooler inside the long building. The owner had built his business out of money spent by the riders from the Heart Circle and the Bar N. When Cal had first shipped in his farmers the sodmen had had a little money to spend in the saloon. Then, with the drought, their money supply low, the farmers had had to stay out of the Down Ace.

The temper of the proprietor had risen with the amount of money the nesters had to spend in his saloon. At first, when money was looser, he had been very cordial to the farmers. But when their money became scarcer, and less was spent for drinks, the proprietor's cordiality had gradually disappeared.

Now, shuffling behind the bar, he hardly paid any attention to Cal. Cal noticed the man's whole attention was on Jack Hutchinson.

"Somethin,' Hutchinson?"

"Two beers."

The man drew the beers, slid them out, picked up the coins. Then he retreated to the end of the bar.

"Not very sociable," Hutchinson murmured.

Cal said quietly, "He don't cotton to me. I'm with the farmers. They're broke; I'm broke. A broke man can't buy drinks."

"To a big long rainy spell," Hutchinson said.

They drank. Cal offered to buy but the superintendent said he had enough. He had some work to do down at the depot. Cal and he went out into the blistering sunshine, and Jack Hutchinson went to the depot.

Cal went over to the blacksmith's shop. Jimmy was sitting on a chair in the shade watching the smithy work. Cal caught the paleness of the youngster's face, although Jimmy showed him a wide smile.

"This is the life, Cal. Here I sit an' watch the other gink work. This bein' a cripple is all right."

"Yeah, for a while. But it'll get tiresome."

Jimmy looked up. "You didn't find no evidence out on that grade, did you?"

"I told you once, no, Jimmy, you just forget those thoughts. You're still a sick kid."

Jimmy was silent. The smithy looked up from his forge. Sweat was dark beads on his sooty forehead. "Oughta have this rig out by tomorrow night, Cal. Any hurry?"

"No hurry, smithy."

Cal got a bronc, and, despite the heat, he rode out into the basin. He had some wheat stored in a granary and he checked this. The bin-door was still locked as Jimmy had left it after he had loaded the grain-tank. Cal figured he had about five hundreds bushels in there yet. Well, when the grain-tank got fixed, he'd load it and haul it into town and sell it.

But he'd do the hauling. And he'd have four

or five farmers riding gun-guard over the rig. Then let either Pete Glenn or Paul Malone hit the rig and try to dump the wheat!

He was riding in the shade of the cotton-woods along Puma river when he met Eddie Malone who rode a lineback buckskin. She made a pretty picture—sunlight glistening on red hair, sitting that big buckskin. Cal's hat came down and he wished he dared tell her how pretty she looked.

"Hot day to ride, Miss Eddie."

She admitted it was. But she had some three-year-old steers that kept grazing along the river despite her efforts to keep them in the foothills where grass was longer.

"With the river so low, the bog-holes are bad. So far I haven't found those steers, either."

"Maybe they went into the hills themselves."

"If they did, it's the first time." She played with the lash on her quirt. "You out cheering up your sodmen?"

"Checking things."

She turned the buckskin. "I don't think you need to fear the Heart Circle, Mr. Rutherford. Mother and I have been working on one Paul Malone rather diligently. We've got him afraid of his own shadow."

Cal held back his smile. Nobody was scaring out Paul Malone. Malone had whipped redskins to keep his herds in Puma Valley.

"I've got to face the cards." Cal Rutherford spoke softly. "There are two cowmen and neither wants nesters in. Your father is one of these cowmen. If I find out who slugged Jimmy and almost killed him by sending that grain-wagon over the cliff—" Cal caught himself.

Eddie said angrily, "Then my word is no good?"

Cal liked her when she was angry. But he didn't tell her. He said, "Both your father and Pete Glenn are under suspicion. They have to be until they prove themselves. Look at it from my viewpoint."

"Your viewpoint seems rather out of line to me."

She turned her buckskin and loped away. Cal watched her for a moment, then rode toward town. He had figured, when first meeting her, he had had a little luck this day. But even that had turned into trouble.

8

SLEEP was a dark blanket wrapping him. But something was disturbing this darkness, smashing it to one side. Cal Rutherford sat up in bed. Because of the heat, he slept naked on top of the covers. Now he sat in the darkness.

"Who's there?"

"Jack Jones."

"What's the matter?"

"Paul Malone's cut my fence on my oats field! I rode out about midnight 'cause the missus said she thought she heard a steer bawl. There was a bunch of Malone steers in my oats!"

Cal was pulling on his pants. The levis were hot against his legs. He jerked on his socks and boots, slid into his shirt. Then he opened the door and lit the lamp.

"Sure they're Malone's stock?"

Jack Jones was angry. "By Gad, Cal, I can read a brand, even if I have to hold a lantern up to it. We cornered one of the buggers, the woman an' me, an' the lantern showed the Heart Circle iron on him!"

"Where are the steers now?"

"We corralled 'em." Jack Jones spat tobacco juice. "An' we aims to hol' 'em until Malone pays us damage for that oats. That's the only crop I had chances of collectin' on, 'cause I got it in so early it made heads before the drought set in. He'll pay plenty."

Cal was ready for the trail. This had him somewhat puzzled. Coming out of such a deep sleep, he still did not have his brain working at top speed. "Are you sure those wires were cut, Jack? The steers didn't just rub down your fence, did they? They'll walk right over a fence when they're hungry enough."

"I got eyes, Cal."

Evidently Jack Jones was in anything but a good humor. And for this, Cal could hardly blame him.

"What's goin' on out there?"

Jimmy's voice came from the other room. Cal hollered "Keep your mug closed, kid, and go back to sleep!"

"What's the matter?"

Cal slammed the door, the safety catch going shut with a metallic snap. He didn't want

Jimmy trying to follow them. He kept wondering if Jack Jones wasn't wrong—maybe the steers had rubbed down the fence and maybe the wires had not been cut, as Jones claimed.

Cal saddled his bronc while Jack Jones sat his horse and waited. There was a lot here that the elevator-man did not understand. He remembered his talk with Eddie Malone and how she had mentioned her prize steers. He judged, from Jack Jones' statements, these were the steers in Jones' oats.

Had either Paul Malone or a Heart Circle rider put those steers into that field? In one night the steers could eat the oats down. But still this didn't make sense Malone surely must have known that, when the steers were discovered in the field, Jack Jones would pen them and hold them for damage fees.

For Jones had this privilege. The steers had destroyed his field, and before he turned them loose again on open range he had the right to hold them until Malone paid for the destruction they had caused. This was the law of the range.

"Malone should have more sense than that," Cal said.

The lamplight streamed through the suddenly

opened door of the office and Jimmy Stephens came out on crutches. Cal told him what had happened and the youth wanted to ride along. Cal knew he could not make the trip.

"You watch the elevator," he said. "That's your job, kid."

"I'd like to go with you, Cal." Jimmy cursed a little. "But I reckon you're right." He crutched back inside, slammed the door, and blew out the kerosene lamp.

Cal's bronc reared, pulling at the bit; the elevator-man gave him his head. They left town at a lope with Jack Jones' cayuse thundering a pace behind Cal's horse. And Cal Rutherford still kept playing with his thoughts.

He still couldn't convince himself it was logical that Paul Malone or a Heart Circle man should cut a fence to run in these steers. For by so doing, Malone would have to pay expenses to Jack Jones. But if the steers had rubbed down the fence—.

That was a different matter. That put a different light on the whole thing. For if the steers could get through the fence, that was the fault of the fence—not the fault of the steers. This range had no herdlaw. You fenced out cattle. And if your fences were weak and cattle went through them—that was just your hard luck.

If Malone's cattle had broken through the fence, that was a sign Jack Jones' fence was weak. In that case, Malone did not have to pay stray-fees. Cal debated this thing mentally at some length. Finally he decided maybe Jones was wrong. Maybe the fence had not been cut. Maybe the Heart Circle cattle had broken in through a poor fence.

Then he remembered that Jones always kept good fences. Well, he could tell something when he arrived at the broken-down fence. When fence-pliers cut a wire they always left marks. When a wire broke of its own accord it just severed. But if pliers cut it—well, it was easy to tell the difference.

The wind was hot. There was a wisp of a moon. Stars looked cold in the cloudless sky. Dust rose from the trail and was powder in Cal's nostrils. Sweat formed around the saddle-blanket and the headstall of his bronc.

"Man, will it ever cool off." Jones breathed the words more as a prayer than a question.

"This winter'll be cool."

Jack Jones cursed. "Sure, it'll be *cold*, not *cool*. Snow miles high and a man's milk-cows standin' there, freezin' an' bawlin' for hay. I oughta get the woman an' household goods an' trek back to Ohiey."

Cal was silent.

"That railroad super—that Jack Hutchinson—he was talkin' to me today, askin' what I wanted for the spread. Claims he aims to buy up some of this land us settlers aim to leave. He says he'll give us a little stake to leave the country on."

"What did you say?"

"I done asked another week. We might get rain, you know. But if it don't rain like fury inside a week, my crops are done ruined. Bob Smith an' Bill Carson an' Ed Stuart aim to peddle to him, I understand."

Cal had a sinking feeling. His own plans, all he had worked for—these were like a house built of cards, and now a harsh hand was toppling them. He didn't know just what to say. He could see Hutchinson's viewpoint. Hutchinson had a little reserve capital to run on: he could wait until irrigation water was brought in from Puma river. By waiting, he would win.

But the farmers had no reserve capital. They were at the ends of their financial ropes. They

95

had wives and children, for the most part; these women and kids had to eat. The drought and the hard winter had sickened them against this land. They had lost their incentives. Cal found himself looking at the sky again. He wished, rather ruefully, that there was some way to make the heavens break out in rain.

"Hang on a while, Jack."

"Why hang on, Cal?" We're whipped. You know it; I know it—we all know it. I had a little hope to make a few dollars with my oats and now those steers—By hades, Paul Malone will pay plenty."

"Maybe Malone didn't cut the fence."

Cal knew instantly he had said the wrong thing.

"I run the best fences in the valley, Cal. Them steers didn't rub down them posts. Cal, don't let that red-head's purty smile turn you against your neighbors!"

"Red-head?"

"You know who I mean—Eddie Malone."

Cal hid his irritation under a long laugh. "Why do you say that, Jones?"

"Some of the women are blabbin' about her makin' them eyes at you. Looks to me as if you're the only one that's wool-blinded."

Cal had a hot reply, but he held it. There was no use in carrying this conversation any further. Dawn was beginning to streak the sky with long fingers of light. This coming day would be another scorcher, for not a cloud touched the unlimited bowl of blue over them.

"Rider comin'," Cal said.

They pulled in, ponies glad to leave the mad pace. The man rode along the lane toward them, and when they got closer Cal recognized him as John Shane, a man who had recently come to Puma City. Shane hung around the Down Ace and gambled quite a bit.

He was a quiet man, thick of shoulder and thigh, and he wore good clothes. Cal had judged him as a professional gambler. They had talked a number of times and John Shane had asked many questions: how was the farming venture turning out, did the farmers have enough money to tide them over until water came into irrigation ditches?

Cal had told the gambler all the trouble confronting himself and the farmers. There was no use in keeping anything private on this range. Everybody knew the predicament he and his hoemen were in.

"So the railroad won't advance no more

money, huh, Rutherford? Well, that's rough, but them big corporations have no heart."

John Shane had gone over to a far table and got in a poker game with Pete Glenn and Marfa Jordan and a few other townsmen. Now, coming upon the gambler in this country lane, with dawn reaching into the sky behind them, Cal Rutherford wondered just why John Shane rode this road.

"You ride in a hurry," Shane said.

Jack Jones demanded, "What're you—a gambler—doin' out here in the farmin' country at dawn, Shane?"

The question was roughly put. But Jack Jones was not noted for his subtlety. Cal wondered what John Shane's answer would be. By rights, the gambler had every qualification for giving back a hot retort. Cal figured each man's business was his own . . . until it interfered with some other citizen's life.

"Is it your business, Jones?"

"A bunch of Malone Heart Circle cattle were put through a cut fence into my oats field," Jones growled. "I'm suspicious of any rider who's out this night."

John Shane looked from Jack Jones over to

Cal Rutherford. Cal noticed a smile touch the man's lips.

"I don't work for the Malone spread," John Shane reminded him gently. "Good morning, gentlemen."

Shane lifted his bronc to a lope, continuing on toward Puma City. Jack Jones turned in saddle and watched the man ride away. "I can't figger this out, Cal. He's a gambler. He ain't got no call to ride this lane at dawn thisaway."

"His business," Cal reminded him.

Jones spat. "Maybe I did jump off the handle, Cal. Well, we better shove ahead. Be daylight when we reach my farm."

They gave their broncs the spurs. Cal let Jack Jones set the pace this time. For some reason, the elevator-owner kept remembering John Shane. Jones was right. Shane had no call to ride range this hour . . . or any other hour.

Then Cal dismissed these thoughts.

Dawn was clear when they reached the fence. Cal Rutherford went down and carefully looked at the severed wires. He remained on one knee for a long moment, looking at the steers in the oats.

They were good steers—three-years-olds—and they packed Paul Malone's Heart Circle iron. They had destroyed the oats field. What they had not eaten, they had trampled down.

"What'd you say about them wires, Cal?"

"They've been cut!"

9

PAUL MALONE'S jowls were as red as Puma River clay. He stared at them, cheeks puffed with anger, almost unable to speak. He looked from Cal Rutherford back to Jack Jones.

"Am I hearin' rightly?"

Jack Jones said, "I reckon you are, Malone. Your steers done et up my oats. What they didn't graze, they tramped down. Somebody cut the fence and choused them in there last night."

Paul Malone caught himself. Some of the color receded from his thick jowls. "Some of you sodbusters got right poor fences," the cowman pointed out. "Mebbe the steers just busted down the fence."

Cal spoke. "Looks to me like the wires were cut, Paul."

Malone looked at the hot sky. "My Gawd, what a way to start what seemed like a nice day. Do I look that loco, men? Credit me with some brains, anyway."

Cal knew what the cowman was driving at but Jack Jones said, "I don't foller you, Malone."

"You don't follow me? You got a head made outa stovewood, sodman? Why would I cut your fence and drive in my cattle? It'd just cost me as much as if I outright bought your oats crop. Now you got my cattle an' I have to pay for the oats. Does it seem logical I cut a fence, drive in my cattle, an' then pay your price for your oats crop?"

"I ain't been paid yet."

"You'll get paid . . . If I'm sure that fence was cut. Now who in hades would cut that fence? Have I got a traitor in my crew?" The cowman turned and stalked toward the bunkhouse where his men were gathering for morning chuck. When he barged in, his hands were eating. He stood for a long moment, jowls jerking in anger, and looked at his cowhands.

One man looked up. "What's wrong, Paul?"

"All you buckos in bed last night?"

Every man there looked up. One puncher asked, "What is this—my ol' unhappy home? My pappy used to check on me, too."

"This ain't nothin' to joke about." Malone told about his steers getting into Jack Jones' oats field. "Somebody cut them wires. Both Jones an' Cal Rutherford says they were cut. Anybody here cut them an' haze them cattle in there?"

Men looked at each other in surprise. Finally the foreman said, "That wouldn't make sense, Paul. I can vouch for every man here. Every one hit soogans last night. Want me to ride with you?"

"I can ride alone." Malone spoke gruffly. "But there might be somebody workin' for Pete Glenn here in this bunch, an' besides drawin' Glenn's wages, he draws mine too. If such is the case, sooner or later I'll find out who he is."

Malone stomped out, talking to himself. He came back to Cal and Jack Jones. "Foreman claims not a man-jack left this spread last night. You didn't ask me, but I'd say Pete Glenn or some of his hands cut that fence an' hazed in my steers. Glenn an' me have rubbed horns a lot lately."

"That don't make sense either," Cal pointed out.

Paul Malone stood rigid, one boot in stirrup. "Why don't it? Glenn wants things to look bad for me. He cut Jones fence an' hazes in my steers. It's as simple as all that . . . to me, anyway."

Cal pointed out that Glenn was no fool. Had Pete Glenn put the steers in the pasture, he would not have cut the fence—he'd have only pushed it down enough to let the steers walk over, thereby making it look as if the steers had themselves rubbed down the fence.

"This does look too simple," Paul Malone said.

Eddie came out of the house. "Where you going, Dad?"

Malone hollered, "You stay home, you red-headed hellion!"

And Cal grinned as they loped out. When Cal looked back, Eddie stood on the steps watching them. He waved, but she did not wave back.

Malone set a wicked pace, driving his fresh bronc through the heat. The tired cayuses of Cal and Jack Jones were hard put to stay close to the mount of the irate cowman. Both Cal and Jones were wondering if Paul Malone told the truth. To Cal, the cowman's words had seemed genuine.

He remembered Malone's surprise when Jones had told about the steers in the oats field. He had carefully watched the cowman. And this had been certain: either Malone had not known about the steers, or else the cowman had been a good actor. And Cal figured the former reason was the motivation of Malone's surprise.

He found himself hoping Malone was not involved in this. He had figured, for some time, that Eddie and Gertrude Malone would keep Paul Malone to be a man of good sense, despite the cowman's violent temper.

Was it because of Eddie that he hoped her father was innocent of this? Riding through the dust, Cal Rutherford pondered with this thought. And he knew it was, in a way, part of his reasoning.

The girl had never given him the slightest tumble. But for some reason he felt she was interested in him. He had been so busy trying to locate farmers and getting Puma Valley under the plough, he had had little time for thoughts of any woman. He wondered if he wouldn't have to change his plans slightly.

This break between Pete Glenn and Paul Malone was not new to him. He knew that the two outfits had tangled over grazing land and waterholes. Not serious arguments, but there had been the smoke of friction. He wondered if Glenn had hazed Malone cattle on to Jack Jones's oats.

Mentally, Cal Rutherford reviewed his predicament. He had to find out somehow who had waylaid Jimmy Stephens, beaten him, then run the grain-tank off the cliff. So far he had made no progress in that direction. He had almost abandoned the hope of getting money from the railroad company for the farmers. This was a sickening thought, but maybe it would not be realized. Maybe rain would come.

Therein lay the futility of the whole thing. It depended upon Nature, and not upon man. And a man had no control over Nature. Jack Hutchinson was trying to buy up the farmers who wanted to leave. Hutchinson would work for the irrigation system, once he owned enough land. Cal had a section of land in the valley. He would, at all costs, hang onto that land, he decided.

But he didn't want Hutchinson owning all the land. Somewhere, Hutchinson was getting some backing; it took dinero—and lots of it—to buy up these farmers. Who was backing Hutchinson?

Somewhere, there was a skunk in the nest-box. From somewhere came a faint, flickering light, it centered, for some reason, around Jack Hutchinson. Cal shut it to one side. He put his mind on what lay ahead.

Paul Malone slacked his pace slightly. Cal drove abreast him. The cowman looked at the elevator-owner.

"I might have an answer to this, Cal."

Jack Jones had run his lathered horse up even, too. Cal caught the hardness of the farmer's eyes as Jones looked at Malone.

"What is it?" Cal asked.

Malone looked at Jones. "Might be that some of your neighbors is drawin' pay from Pete Glenn to raise hell among you folks. Might be this hired son has cut this fence an' hazed in my steers to make it look bad for me."

"Might be you did it yourself, too," Jones retorted.

Paul Malone's right fist balled hard. Cal thought the cowman intended to knock the farmer from saddle. Again Jack Jones' mouth had got him into trouble. Cal said hurriedly, "Don't, Malone."

"Let him come ahead," Jones invited sullenly. "I kin whup him at marbles, cards or fists."

But good humor had Paul Malone by now.

"I get enough fightin' at home with the woman an' Eddie, without lookin' for more away from home."

The heat had taken the run from their broncs and they settled to a long trot. The rest of the distance was ridden in silence. Malone was quiet, braced against stirrups, riding high in leather with his big hands locked across the fork of his kak. Jack Jones was scowling, fighting his thoughts.

And Cal Rutherford was mulling over Paul Malone's theory. And he was finding much meat in it. Maybe one of his farmers was a traitor and was working with Pete Glenn. Malone had hit upon something substantial; yet Cal hoped it were not true. A traitor was a low-down animal. Even the thought, to Cal Rutherford, was repulsive. He didn't like it one bit.

One by one, he checked his farmers; he probed into their characters, their weaknesses, their strengths. And not a one could he lay a mental finger upon. Finally he gave up and figured Malone was wrong.

But was the cowman in error?

A man never knew about his fellow-men. A man presumably your friend could talk nice to you, pretend to work with you, and all the time he could secretly be working against you, betraying you, violating each step forward you took. That was one of the dirty deals of life. Cal Rutherford had long ago recognized this tenet of life. He had recognized it and then apparently ignored it.

Any man was honest to him until that man, through tongue or deed, proved himself otherwise. This philosophy, Cal knew, was sound. Yet for once he decided to violate it. He would watch and listen and some of these farmers would be considered false until they proved themselves otherwise.

He was sure Paul Malone had not cut the fence. He fingered his swollen lip. Marfa Jordan and he had not met since their fight. He wondered what would happen when he met the Glenn gunhand again. The weight of his .45 on his right hip was not reassuring.

He did not like guns. Guns were from a barbaric age where men fought with weapons and not reason. He knew how to handle a gun; so did Marfa Jordan. When they met the thought was almost repulsive.

Yet he had resigned himself to this thought. He would not give an inch against Jordan. Nor would he draw back from Glenn, either. The last few days—these days with their wildness and trouble—had changed his mind about lots of things.

"Hutchinson is buying up the farmers," he told Malone.

Malone looked at him in puzzlement. "He's no farmer. He's a railroad man. I don't savvy it."

"Aims to hold the land until water comes in ditches. Wish I had some cash and I'd buy some of the property."

"You hold notes for the money you lent them, don't you?"

Cal smiled. "Yes, but the sums are small. Hutchinson will pay them and then they'll pay me."

"Wonder Pete Glenn doesn't buy some."

"I've wondered about that point, too. I've asked around, but Pete Glenn ain't made anybody any offers."

Malone nodded.

Cal asked, "Why don't you tie onto some land?"

Malone shook his head. "I've got all I can handle. I've made up my mind not to fight the farmers, Cal. Eddie an' Ma talked the law into

110

me. I've got all the stock I want, and if farmers cut into the valley land more, I trek back into the hills. Wyomin' didn't stop farmers. Neither can I. I'm no ploughman. Farmin' holds nothin' for me. I'm a saddle-man.''

Jack Jones had been listening. "By hades, Malone, you talk sense, fella. I'm beginnin' to believe you mebbe didn't cut my fence. Mebbe you was jobbed, at that." The farmer rubbed his jaw and spat tobacco-juice.

Malone winked at Cal, who grinned.

They reached the fence and went down. Malone looked at the steers and at the ruined oats field. He walked over to the wires and looked at them. Jack Jones and Cal followed the cowman.

Malone rolled a wire between thumb and forefinger, studying the broken end. He dropped that one and picked up another and repeated the process. Cal watched the cowman's face become blunt and hard.

"They've been cut, all right. Cut with wire-cutters, looks like."

Jack Jones nodded. Cal was silent.

Malone walked out into the oats. They had been trampled rather badly. He pulled off a few heads and studied them.

"I'll make you a deal, Jones. You cut this hay and stack it for me and I'll pay you five bucks an acre."

Jones rubbed his jaw. "Six bucks, Malone."

Malone grinned at Cal. "You never can please people, Rutherford. All right, we split the difference. Five-fifty per acre?"

Jones sent an inquiring glance at Cal, who nodded.

"It's a deal," Jones said.

10

THAT night Marfa Jordan came into the Bar N astraddle a steel-dust gelding showing plainly the dust and tiredness of a long hard ride. He put the steel-dust in the barn after watering him at the trough. He jerked off his saddle, threw the sweat-wet blanket over the stall partition, and went toward the house where the light burned low behind the shade.

He did not knock.

It was hot in the living-room. He stood for a moment with the shadows washing and playing across his swollen, beaten face. The night had been hot, the ride long, but this room was even hotter. But he just stood there and he said, "Pete. Pete Glenn."

Silence.

"Pete."

Then, "Coming."

Glenn wore a silk dressing-gown pulled over silk pyjamas. He looked citified and sleek, and Jordan noticed the man had combed his hair before coming out of his bedroom. This registered on the gunhand, drawin' a fine thin line of disdain, for Marfa Jordan had made his way with cattle and with dust, and Glenn had always hired somebody to clear his way. But this feeling was not long with Jordan. He knew that, underneath, beneath this citified, smooth exterior, Pete Glenn was tough, and when he had to face the dust—he faced it.

"Well, Jordan?"

Glenn always spoke that way. Sort of patronizin' and overbearing, no matter where the place or the time or the circumstance. For the thousandth odd time, this rubbed against Marfa Jordan, and for the thousandth odd time, Jordan decided not to notice it.

"Them Heart Circle steers are grazin' in Jack Jones' oats right now, Glenn."

"You took a long time."

That was Pete Glenn again! He didn't say, "That's good," nor did he say, "A job well done." He was always ahead of you.

"I circled into the hills for the lava beds. Was afraid somebody might trail. That made it a long circle."

"That was needless. Nobody can trail in a lane cut up by hoofs. Did anybody see you?"

Marfa Jordan showed his teeth in a difficult smile, for his lips were heavy from Cal Rutherford's fists. "I'm here without a bullet-hole. Had anybody caught sight of me, they'd been gunfire, huh?"

"You pushed the fence down?"

"I had to cut it."

Pete Glenn looked at his gunman. He was very, very quiet. He was too quiet. The lamplight showed from his blue-shaven jaw. Marfa Jordan watched him. Jordan's big-knuckled hands moved a little along the brim of the gunman's Stetson. They moved with slow uncertainty.

"You cut it?"

Jordan said, "That fence was new. Good diamond-willow posts that wouldn't break. I tried to jerk them out with my hoss an' rope, but they was too solid. That wire was strung tight an' it held, too."

"Then you cut it?"

"Yeah, with my wire-cutters."

Jordan kept watching Glenn. Pete Glenn was not looking at his gunman now. He was watching the low-turned flame of the kerosene lamp on the oak dining-room table. He was watching it with the fierce intensity a snake uses when he watches a mouse-hole.

There seemed, then, to be only one thing of interest in the world to Pete Glenn; that interest was the lamp-flame. But Marfa Jordan, because he knew this cowman, knew of Glenn's pride and strength and greed, knew this was only a pose to hide thoughts inside.

The silence grew and it gained weight and structure. It grew to almost visible weight. Jordan was the first to speak.

"I had to cut the fence or the cattle'd never got into them oats."

"Forget it, Jordan."

Jordan said, "I knowed mebbe it wasn't right. I knowed by cuttin' them wires it might not look like them cattle got in there by themselves. But I still figure Jack Jones will make Paul Malone pay for it."

Pete Glenn's voice was very dry. It sounded like two dry corn bogs running together. "That's where you did wrong." He was a father speaking to an errant little boy. He needed Marfa Jordan's guns. He had already make up his mind that Jordan's brain was impossible. "We don't want Jack Jones to get dinero from Malone. We wanted Jones to lose his oats and then be broke and then leave the country after selling out to Hutchinson for a few cents on a dollar. You balled the whole thing up. Now we gotta sit back and just watch and keep our mouths shut. Remember that, Jordan: *Keep your mouth shut*."

"Malone might not pay."

"I think he will. Paul Malone has two women working on him night and day. If he was alone, he'd probably fight. But with those women—. Still, you did some good. Those others will be a-scared and will sell out sooner to Hutchinson."

"How about this Hutchinson? He's slippery. He's playin' a fast game, too. Can we trust him?"

Pete Glenn took his gaze away from the lamp. He said, very clearly, very crisply, "That's my business."

Marfa Jordan showed his anger. But he turned and went outside and went into the bunk-house. The heat of early forenoon sifted through the ceiling and brought sweat to his coarse body and awoke him. He went outside to where the men had a barrel of water suspended against the building. He pulled the spotcord rope and water sprayed from the can with the holes cut into it. Jordan got soap and lathered it into the wool of his hairy body.

The windmill squeaked as the fan turned in the slow lazy wind. It seemed to protest against working in this heat. Jordan could see a corral, and horses stood there under the shade of the cottonwood tree that branched out and almost covered the enclosure with shade. Horses stood silent and switched at flies and occasionally stomped against heel-flies.

The gunman washed the soap from his body and wiped on a towel that had once been cleaner. For a moment, with the breeze against the dampness of his body, he felt coolness; this dried and the breeze was hot. He dressed and went to the barn and Pete Glenn came out of the shadows.

"Get a fresh horse, Marfa."

"Where to?"

"Puma City."

Glenn had his horse saddled; he waited. Marfa Jordan took a pinto—a gaudy black and white horse—but tough to the trail. He lifted his kak and cinched it, and he was tired as he swung up.

"Heat ahead," he said.

"Heat is our friend," Pete Glenn reminded.

"Heck of a friend."

They rode at a lope until their broncs got too hot; then they reined to a walk. A fast walk a cowboy calls a running-walk. Neither spoke on the ride into Puma City. Jordan was hot and miserable and wished he had not taken the bath —it made him feel even hotter.

"Kids," Glenn said.

They were on Puma City's outskirts. Town boys were swimming in a pot-hole in the river. Jordan looked as one boy, naked, dived from the bank. Jordan said, "Them was the days, Pete."

"You think so?"

Jordan looked at him. "I know so."

Pete Glenn said, "Not for me, friend. Lazy days they were, without purpose; only an occasional fist-fight to break them. Some people want to go back. I don't. I liked them but I'd never want them again."

Jordan listened.

"I like trouble, Marfa. I like to get in and work and use my head, and when my head won't carry me through there's my gun."

Jordan asked, "How about this Cal Rutherford?"

"When we get done here, Rutherford will be

broke. He's got a little wheat left out in that granary. Not much. He's got his elevator almost clear. But when we get done, he'll wish he'd've burned his elevator. 'Cause it'll be owned by Jack Hutchinson and Pete Glenn."

Marfa Jordan rubbed his hand on his saddle-horn.

"Maybe it'll be owned just by Pete Glenn," the Bar N owner corrected.

Now Marfa Jordan smiled. "That would be best," he admitted. He was thinking of something. ". . . he'll wish he'd've burned his elevator . . . wheat . . . out in that granary . . ." Marfa Jordan hated Cal Rutherford. Marfa Jordan kept on thinking and remembering.

They rode into the town livery and went down. The hostler took their broncs, and Pete Glenn said, "We stick close together, see. First, I've got to see Jack Hutchinson. He'll be down the depot. You go to the Down Ace and stay there."

"Paul Malone's bronc was in that barn," Marfa Jordan pointed out. "So was the cayuse belongin' to that nester Jack Jones. Yonder behind the livery barn is Cal Rutherford's nag."

"Just sit a tight saddle."

Marfa Jordan went on toward the Down Ace.

Jack Hutchinson sat in the depot-office, both windows open, shirt unbuttoned, boots on his desk. Outside, the operator's key kept up its incessant chatter.

"What's new, Jack?"

Hutchinson turned his body slightly in the swivel-chair but did not drop his boots. Pete Glenn shut the door behind him and stood with his back to the door, looking at the railroad superintendent.

"That oats field," Hutchinson said. "Jordan bungled that. Malone is in town with Jack Jones to get money from the bank to pay Jones."

"Jordan's shy of brains." Glenn held a brief smile.

"Get rid of him."

Glenn shook his head. He was deliberate and slow. "He slings a fast gun. He might mean the difference between life and the black for one Pete Glenn. This isn't going to run long. Somebody'll wise up. Then there'll be a little thing called gunsmoke. It all ends this way. No man's tracks can be covered."

"You afraid?"

The question was blunt and rough. It smashed into Pete Glenn and pulled blood from his lips and brought his lower lip under his teeth. He stood like that for a long moment, and the color pulled back into his blocky face again.

"Don't rub me, Hutchinson."

Hutchinson returned to looking out the window. Pete Glenn stood and looked at the railroad man; outside, the key kept talking. It was a metallic sound, sharp and without sense to Glenn. The wind came in the window, and it was hot and without reason. It ruffled Hutchinson's loose shirt.

"We've got to get rid of Rutherford," Glenn said quietly. "I've tried to get him to walk into Marfa Jordan's gun, but it turned out in a fist-fight and Jordan got the worst."

"Rutherford packs a gun now."

Pete Glenn gave this thought. "We got to match him with somebody and get him killed off. With him gone these farmers will drift out pronto. There should be some way to put him against Paul Malone."

"I doubt it."

"Why?"

"Malone and Rutherford and Jones just rode into town together. Malone has a red-headed daughter. A woman can work wonders over a man, Glenn."

Pete Glenn said, "There must be a way." He was making no progress here. He was ahead of Hutchinson . . . or so he hoped. When the time came and this was won and Hutchinson was used . . . then Hutchinson would go. Of his own accord or under a gun or anyway—just to get rid of him. This basin did not have room for two men to boss it. But that time was ahead.

He went outside, walking through the heat, and he met Paul Malone. And Pete Glenn said, "Heard your steers got you into some trouble, Paul."

Malone told him about Jones' oats.

"Maybe Jones turned them in there himself."

Malone said, "Explain further huh?"

Glenn said, "I don't like to say this, Paul, but you seem to take men too much at their face value. The scheme isn't hard to see through. Rutherford and Jones could have cooked it up."

"Keep on."

Glenn smiled. "You can see through it, can't you?"

"Rutherford and Jones cut that fence. They herded in my steers to make me pay a bill. Is that what you're headin' at, Pete?"

"That's it."

"I'm still a jump ahead of you." Malone went

toward the barn. Pete Glenn smiled and went to the Down Ace. He was at the corner of the block when he heard the bullet roar.

He counted three shots, all evenly spaced. He wondered if Marfa Jordan had tangled guns with Cal Rutherford. Then he saw Rutherford coming on the run from his elevator.

A man came out of the saloon, wild with haste. Pete Glenn grabbed him. "What happened?"

"This Jack Jones, he got purty drunk. Malone paid him in cash for that oats field."

"What else?"

"Well, Marfa Jordan was in there. Jones got loose-tongued an' said maybe Jordan had hazed in them steers. Lots of it don't make sense to me."

It made sense to Pete Glenn, though. But he held this behind a stern face. "They went for their guns?"

"Jones got in one shot. Your man got in two. Now get your hand off me, Glenn. I gotta get Doc."

"Here he comes now."

11

CAL RUTHERFORD said, "Jones left a woman and a boy. Reckon the kid must be about three or there abouts."

"Tough on them," John Shane said.

The elevator-man and the gambler stood in the shade of the Down Ace. Two men had just carried Jack Jones' body across the street to the shack used as Puma City's morgue. Jones' head lopped; his body was sagging and limp. Cal kept remembering back a few hours. He and Jones had inspected that cut fence, had ridden over to talk with Paul Malone . . . Jack Jones had been alive then; he'd responded to heat and words and movements.

Maybe Cal's face showed his sorrow. For John Shane said, "Nothing a man can do for the dead. They're out of this wild mess and maybe they're better off." Doc Wilson tooled a team of sorrels and a buckboard out of the alley. "Doc's going out to break the news to Mrs. Jones. That isn't a nice job."

Cal watched the medico leave town. He

125

looked at the Down Ace. From inside came voices—Pete Glenn, Jack Hutchinson, Paul Malone, other influential local men. They were questioning Marfa Jordan. Cal could hear the mumble of their voices but could not make out their words.

"I was in a poker game," John Shane said. "Jordan is clear with the law, such as it is around here. Jones was drinking. He bumped into Jordan—or maybe Jordan bumped into him—and they had words. Jones went for his gun and Jordan gave him time and then Jordan killed him."

"Jordan made it look like self-defense?"

Shane nodded. "That gunman is smart. He's fast, too." The gambler gave this thought dull consideration. "But I've seen them faster." Shane turned a slow glance on Cal Rutherford. "This range might get awful hot now that a farmer has been killed by a cattleman gunhand. . . ."

Cal admitted the farmers might be hard to hold. He did not want to see Puma Valley turn into a red hell of guns and powdersmoke. John Shane wondered if it wasn't best that the farmers get assembled in a meeting and talk this over. Cal admitted he had been thinking of such a plan.

I'm goin' to ride out an' get them together tonight at the schoolhouse. I'd best get Jack Hutchinson to help me, I reckon. He's the railroad representative and he's got lots of influence."

John Shane nodded, seemingly indifferent. Cal realized the gambler had nothing at stake here in Puma Valley. This recent killing—and this trouble—was probably interesting to John Shane, but meant nothing beyond a cursory interest. Shane had no farm or woman or kids on this grass.

Nevertheless, Cal Rutherford found himself liking this quiet, thick-shouldered man. For some reason, he and John Shane seemed to hit it off well together. Now John Shane said, "I'm going back into the saloon. I'll tell Hutchinson you want to see him."

"I'll go inside, too."

Shane gave him a long, slow look, and Cal knew what the gambler thought. Marfa Jordan was in there, and Jordan had just killed, and Cal had beaten Jordan down with his fists. Then Shane shrugged. "Your funeral, Rutherford."

They went into the darkened saloon. The

odors of beer and whisky were stale and so strong they seemed almost to possess definite outlines. A few townsmen sat at the gaming tables, but they did not play cards. They were listening to the talk between the men and Marfa Jordan.

Jordan stood with his back to the bar and with his questioners in front of him. He looked at Cal Rutherford but apparently did not see him. Cal knew this was just a pose, nothing more.

"That's all there was to it," Jordan said. "He pulled his gun, and I gave him a chance, and it was either him or me." He added, "Some of these blasted farmers are plenty sprucy. They walk like they own the town."

Pete Glenn looked at Jack Hutchinson. "You and Cal Rutherford got these farmers in. You've heard Jordan's version of this. Other onlookers have testified Jack Jones pulled first. You satisfied?"

"Self-defense," Hutchinson said.

Glenn looked at Cal Rutherford. "An' you, Rutherford?"

"Words can't bring a dead man on his feet. The thing I've got to work against now is that these farmers don't move against you cowmen. That'd mean death on both sides."

"All my men are armed," Pete Glenn said. "So are Paul Malone's men. Those hoemen of yours would find it tough going, Rutherford."

"You talk like you want war."

Glenn shook his head gently. "I don't want war. But if it comes the Bar N don't run." He turned to the bar. "Have a drink, Paul?"

"Not today," Cal heard Malone say. "My belly don't set just right. Reckon I'll trek on home."

Cal caught Jack Hutchinson's eye and they went outside. The elevator-man told about his plan to get the farmers to meet. Hutchinson agreed with him. He would ride out and tell the farmers about the meeting.

"Marfa Jordan had orders to kill Jack Jones," Cal said. "I can't prove it but I know darned well Pete Glenn told him to kill Jones. Glenn wants trouble here. He wants these farmers to pull out. Then he can rip down fences and run his cattle in on the land they once owned."

"That's quite an accusation," Hutchinson said.

Cal caught himself. He shrugged, spread his hands. "Looks that way to me, Hutchinson.

129

Fact is, I figure Glenn would like to buy the farmers out, one at a time, but none will deal with him—they hate his guts."

Hutchinson looked at him. "That would be a good hand for either Glenn or Malone to play. So far, I've got option on about two sections from the farmers. If they leave I pay them a buck an acre."

"Cheap land."

"Runs into money. A section would cost me six hundred and forty dollars. Then I'd have to wait a few years until this irrigation goes through. Too bad you haven't cash to option some of it, Cal."

"You can't use wood for money."

Hutchinson went to the livery barn for his horse. Cal saw Paul Malone ride out of the barn. Malone saw him and rode over to him. The cowman's face was blunt and bulldoggish.

"This might've pried the lid off trouble, Cal."

Cal told how he and Hutchinson were getting the farmers together that evening. Paul Malone wondered if it would do any good if he rode over and talked to the hoemen. Cal and he talked this over. Both finally decided it was best that Malone stay away from the meeting.

"Them farmers'll be as itchy as a dynamite cap," Cal summed up. "You ride in there and some hothead might pop off his mug an' want to have them tie into you. I'll explain that you paid Jack Jones for the oats your cows got into. But this will be a hard deal for Hutchinson an' me to handle."

"Sure hate to see a shootin' war crop up, Cal."

"We gotta hold it down," Cal agreed.

Malone touched spurs and loped north into the heat. Cal told Jimmy about the killing of Jack Jones. The seriousness of the situation showed in the youth's quietness.

"Goin' out to get the nesters to meet," Cal said.

"I'd cotton to go along," Jimmy said. "My leg is well now. I walk most of the time without a crutch, Cal."

Cal put his arm around the youth's shoulders. Jimmy had picked up quite a bit of weight. For a moment loneliness was with Cal Rutherford. He was bucking a tough game and it was swell to have somebody who sided him.

"Kid, your job is to watch this elevator. This place would burn like a stack of cards. This thing is getting stiff, Jimmy. Stay close to this building."

"But how about that wheat—out there in your granary?"

Cal told him Ed Stuart was keeping an eye on that granary. Jimmy reminded that Stuart would probably be at the meeting. Then who would watch the granary?

"I'll see Ed today and check on that point. You stay close to this elevator, Jimmy."

"All right, Cal."

Hutchinson rode up when Cal was saddling his horse. He waited until Cal got into leather. They rode through the heat at a walk. Cal outlined their plan of procedure.

"I'll take the south side of Puma River, Hutchinson. You warn the farmers on the north side."

They parted company at Martin's Crossing. Hutchinson waded his horse across the shallow stream, now almost dry because of the drought. Not a single cloud decorated the sky. The sun was merciless.

Cal talked first with Bob Smith. The man was standing in the shade of his cabin, and when Cal rode up he showed a bleak smile.

"That wheat field's got about three more

132

days, I figure. If we don't get rain by then I'm broke. I'll cut it and sell it to one of these cowmen an' lose money on the deal."

Cal told about Jack Jones' death.

Bob Smith's craggy face paled. He rubbed a bony hand across his sweaty forehead. "Dang, but I cottoned to Jones, too. Be hard on his widder an' kid. Yeah, I'll be at the meetin', Cal. The woman'll stay at home an' guard the spread with a rifle. Yeah, I'll be there."

"Eight o'clock."

Bob Smith called, "Sary, come here," and his wife came out of the cabin. Cal rode away. When he glanced back, Smith was talking with his wife. Evidently he was telling her about Jack Jones' passing.

Cal had a wry taste on his tongue. This was harder on the women and children than it was on the men. They had to stay at home and worry and watch. When darkness came this valley would be spiked with rifles and guns. Rifles and guns held in the hands of mothers and wives and children.

While he had expected some opposition from Paul Malone and Pete Glenn, he had not expected this much. Had the railroad not promised to see him through, he would not have brought settlers into Puma Valley. But the railroad had offered to see the farming project through to the stage where irrigation water tumbled down the ditches to run onto land that would suck it in and bring out green and priceless wheat and corn and oats and barley.

He knew resentment was high against him. It was bound to be. This resentment, he figured, was mostly with the women. The men could appreciate his plight. But the women were dissatisfied with him and angry with him.

This hurt more than he cared to admit. It was rubbing him inside, harsh as coarse sand, wearing into him, grinding him down. He had written to the railroad officials—men he had never met—protesting the treatment the railroad had given him in violation of its promises to him and his farmers.

So far, he had received not a word in reply. They were even ignoring his letters. Hutchinson had heard from the board and Hutchinson had shown him the letter. They would act through Hutchinson. Not another cent was forthcoming. The whole deal had been a mistake. According to reports, the United States Department of Interior intended to run water into Puma

Valley. The railroad company would wait until water came.

"They run a whammy over both of us," Jack Hutchinson had said sourly. "These farmers don't cotton to me; I'm division superintendent. Some of them figure sure I haven't worked hard enough for them. But what more could I do?"

"You don't hold the purse-strings," Cal had admitted.

Cal figured Hutchinson was redeeming himself somewhat by purchasing farms from the broke farmers. This gesture had seemed very nice to a few of the sodmen. But it took lots of money to buy up so much land. And it seemed Hutchinson had the dinero.

Bill Carson swore with a methodical regularity upon hearing about Jack Jones' death.

"That was murder, Cal. Plain, cold-blooded murder! What else could it be? Jack Jones weren't no gun-slammer like Marfa Jordan! I sure wished you'd've kilt Jordan in that fistfight!"

"I tried, Bill." Cal rubbed his left elbow. "I hit him so hard I danged near busted my elbow. Well, be at the meetin', huh?"

"I'll be there . . . with my gun."

Ed Stuart took the news with a doggedness

that gave no display of emotion. He was a short, dark-haired man. He shook his head slowly and allowed he'd be at the meeting. Nobody had been pestering Cal's granary. His boy was on guard over there nights. The kid was in the house trying to sleep now.

"A fella can't sleep in this heat, though."

Cal talked with young Bill. He was paying the boy fifty cents a night to watch the wheat. "I'll haul it into town next week. Probably next Tuesday."

"I'll watch it until then, Cal." The boy yawned widely.

Ed Stuart walked to the gate with the elevator man. He related that Jack Hutchinson had offered to buy his land for a dollar an acre. "He seems to have lots of dinero, Cal. Wonder where he gets it?"

"Told me he'd saved some. He also said he'd borrowed some."

Ed Stuart rubbed his stubbed jaw. "I wonder if us farmers are bein' jobbed, Cal? I wonder if we ain't been worked for suckers from the beginnin'."

Cal's face flushed. "Don't accuse me of workin' against you, Stuart!"

Ed Stuart raised a hurried hand. "Now don't

pull at the bit, Cal. You done got me wrong. I don't mean you was in on it. You've been square to us farmers—you got your own dinero invested. But Hutchinson never had a cent invested until the last few weeks."

Cal was silent.

"Mebbeso I'm wrong," Stuart admitted.

Cal said, "I've thought of that, too. But hang it, Ed, it don't seem reasonable. I hate to think that of Hutchinson."

"He could be buyin' land for one of the cowmen on commission. Workin' under the table. He's mighty friendly downtown with Paul Malone. Seen 'em together at the Down Ace a number of times, drinkin'."

Cal reminded him that Hutchinson had been seen many times talking with Pete Glenn, too. Hutchinson worked for the railroad and his job was to help keep peace in Puma Valley.

"I think we're both wrong, Ed."

"I hope so, Cal."

12

THEY came in buggies, in buckboards, in wagons. They came on horseback, and one man drove a mule hitched to a cart. They tied their rigs and animals in the brush along Puma River, for the school's small barn soon held all the horseflesh it could hold.

It was hot.

A sticky, wet river-heat.

Dusk was coating the land. It hung to hills and filled coulees and draws and gave the rimrock a mystic touch. Mosquitoes were thick. They came out of the river bottom. They tortured man and beast alike.

"As if we ain't got enough misery now." A farmer swatted at a pesky mosquito. "A man never can hit one of them things."

There wasn't a woman in the bunch. The women were at home on guard. This was a man's meeting.

Cal Rutherford and Jack Hutchinson had reached the schoolhouse ahead of the farmers. They had taken sticks and made smoke smudges that had driven away most of the mosquitoes. Cal went from man to man, talking and testing opinions. Some of them were rather rebellious.

"You got me into this, Rutherford," Mack Nuggon declared. "Now I'm stuck here in this blasted desert!"

The surliness of Nuggon's voice silenced the surrounding farmers. Somewhere the stomp of a bronc sounded loud. Cal could almost feel the imprint of the eyes on him.

"You've been drinkin' too much, Nuggon."

Cal moved on. Mack Nuggon reached out. Cal felt the man's harsh fingers grip tough into his shoulder. Cal hit and hit hard. Nuggon went back and sat down, and Cal stood over him.

Cal's voice was thin. Yet despite its tightness, it carried far. "You're over twenty-one, Nuggon. You're supposed to be a man. You can vote and you're supposed to be able to think. You're not thinkin' now. You're lettin' your tongue talk, that's all."

Nuggon said, "I'll get up an' I'll—"

Bob Smith said, "Sit down, Nuggon, or I'll knock you down the next time. Cal's in this to his ears, too. Where we got one buck invested, he's got five. Just remember that before you shoot off again!"

Nuggon got up, brushing himself. "I'm sorry, Cal."

"Apology accepted."

Cal heard a man say, "My Gawd, but that man can hit! He walks ahead like a cougar and his fists are a bronc's kicks!"

But there was no lift from the words. He was almost sorry he had knocked down Mack Nuggon. He had acted on impulse, this trouble raw inside of him—it had made him fast and lithe and deadly. Maybe he had profited by it, though.

For one thing, his inner tension was slightly released. The wild flare-up of physical action had broken the stiffness inside of him. But this compensation, such as it was, was meagre.

He had also accomplished something else. Many of these farmers were on the verge of picking trouble with him. They too were nervous and on edge. By knocking down Mack Nuggon he had shown them, in one fast second, he was no sap—he would not take their guff and swallow it. Probably some of them had wondered and doubted his sincerity in this. Now they doubted no longer.

He had hurt the elbow he had injured in his fight with Marfa Jordan. This pain was wry in him, a constant reminder that Jordan was his enemy. But for the time being he put it aside against the measurement of this meeting.

Hutchinson said, "You did right, Cal."

"Only thing I could do, Jack."

Hutchinson sent his gaze across the men. "I reckon they're all here, Cal. We might just as well call the meeting to order."

"All men inside," Cal said.

They trooped into the small schoolhouse. Inside it was as hot as a furnace. One said, "The devil is stockin' lotsa coal tonight," and he sat down and peeled off his shirt. Cal and Hutchinson stood on the slightly raised platform beside the teacher's desk.

"I'll handle it," Cal said.

Hutchinson sat down on a chair and balanced it against the wall. He breathed heavily against the heat and then was silent. Cal used the teacher's pointer-stick as a gavel, rapping the desk with the big end of the hardwood pointer. Silence fell quickly among the farmers.

He looked down at them. He looked at their sun-tanned, weather-lined faces with the yellow, uncertain lamplight flickering across them. For a moment, indecision was his. He had a real task at hand. Could he meet it? Could he conquer it?

"Men," he said. His voice grew stronger. He told them about Jack Jones' death under Marfa Jordan's gun. He reminded them that Jones had drawn first. He stressed the fact that Jones had been under the influence of alcohol.

"I called you together tonight to draw up a plan of action." He held up his hand to silence a man who had started to rise. "And by *action*, I do not mean warfare against the Bar N or Heart Circle."

"They'll kill us, Cal," a man said. "Just like they killed Jack Jones."

Cal asked for patience. "If they move against another one of us, we'll band and carry the fight. But remember that Jones pulled a gun against Marfa Jordan, and Jordan was not the aggressor."

He stressed the fact that Paul Malone had promised he would not move against the farmers.

"That's what Malone says with his mouth," a farmer said. "But what does he do with his fists and the guns of his men? That's a different deal, Cal. Me, I've found my gates down, with

Malone Heart Circle cows grazin' on my wheat. Who but Malone or one of his men let down that gate to let them cows in?"

"Did you see Malone open that gate, Hartley?"

"No, but I reckon he did it. Or had it ordered did."

Cal said, "You have no proof."

One man said, "Do you work for Malone? Is that why you pertect him? Or is it his red-headed daughter—"

Already Cal was moving down the aisle toward the man. He was sick inside, for his scheme was falling apart at the seams, yet this discouraging knowledge did not show in his dark face. They were watching him, craning in seats, twisted on the benches, and they were silent. Cal walked down that aisle, aware of all this. And inside was the hollowness of defeat.

He was the captain, and his crew was in mutiny. He had just knocked down one of the crew, and yet brute force and the display of brute strength did not work. This thought pounded inside of him. It registered, had its knowledge, and then he was abreast of the man, who was standing up.

"Muggins," Cal said, "I want your apology."

Muggins had his fists doubled. He expected to fight. This knowledge was scrawled in tight lines across his thick face. His blue eyes faced Cal and Cal read the hesitation in them. Muggins figured a fight had been ahead, and here Cal had asked his apology.

"I'm sorry, Cal."

Cal said, "Shake hands."

They shook hands, both with firm grips. Cal saw he had handled this better than if he had used force. When he walked back to the desk he heard the dim murmur of whispers. They were eyeing him with new respect.

"We take a vote against war."

Hutchinson wrote on the blackboard. "Those who want to ride against the Bar N and Heart Circle," and below it he wrote, "Those who want to sit tight and watch to see what happens." Cal called a man-to-man vote. Each man stood up and called, "Yes," or "No." The Noes had it. Only one man wanted to ride against Pete Glenn and Paul Malone.

"That's decided," Cal said. He thanked them for their confidence. "Now Jack Hutchinson has a few words."

Hutchinson also pleaded for peace. He stressed the fact the men were family men and had dependents. Any man dissatisfied, he said, could sell out to him. He had faith in this country.

"Why doesn't your railroad have faith in us?" Muggins asked.

Hutchinson pointed out that he only worked for the railroad. He was not on the board of directors. He was a man on a salary. He had worked hard to get his job and gone up slowly, bucking the seniority list.

"I have done all I can. I'll try to do more. Neither Mr. Rutherford nor I have quit fighting."

It was a good talk and it drew applause. Cal realized Hutchinson was a more accomplished speaker than he was. Hutchinson knew how to play upon the logic and nerves of these men.

"Your meeting, Cal."

Again Cal took the makeshift gavel. He said but a few more words. He again asked for faith in him. He was lifting the gavel to adjourn the meeting when two people entered.

The lamplight showed on the craggy face of Paul Malone. It danced across the red hair of Eddie. Cal paused, gavel raised. His surprise was written across his face. Paul Malone and

Eddie used a lot of nerve to enter this bunch of hostile farmers. They were brave.

Eddie smiled at him then—a slow, uncertain smile—and Cal felt a sudden lift. Farmers were staring at the couple. Cal rapped savagely with his gavel. He called for order.

"We have two guests, and that is only proper. We have heard the sides of us farmers in this debate. We would like a few words from Mr. Malone. Will you come forward, Mr. Malone?"

Muggins rapped out. "You staked no gunmen outside, Malone?"

"No gunmen, fella."

Malone moved down the aisle, red-faced and thick of shoulder. Eyes were on him, and they were not friendly. Eddie followed her father. They came up on the platform and Hutchinson said, "Take my chair, Miss Malone." Hutchinson stood up and then moved back and leaned against the wall.

Paul Malone stood behind the desk, with Cal Rutherford to his left. Malone looked for a long moment over the farmers. His gaze went from face to face. Cal watched him. But Malone's heavy face seemingly had no thoughts.

"Friends," Malone began, "my daughter and

my wife asked me to ride here and talk with you."

The cowman talked simply, forcibly. When Jack Jones had been killed, he had taken the money from the corpse—the money he had paid Jones for the oats Heart Circle cattle had trampled.

"I turned that money over to Mrs. Jones, gentlemen. I tell you this only to show you I am honest and want to treat people honestly."

"You talk interestin'," a man scoffed.

Malone's face turned turkey-red. Cal thought the hair-trigger temper would break loose. Only by sheer effort did Malone control his temper. He sleeved his forehead with his shirt-sleeve.

"Gentlemen, if you don't care about what I have to say, my daughter an' me'll leave."

One farmer said, "Stick aroun', Malone. I'll see you have no more interruptions. Parker, you an' me is monitors."

The farmer and a skinny man went into the aisle and walked up and down silently. Malone continued.

He pointed out neither he nor any of his riders had cut Jack Jones' fence to haze in Heart Circle cattle. He stressed the point that he had issued concise orders to his riders there would be no wire-cutting or dropping of gates to let cattle in on the crops of the farmers.

"I make no effort to hold land that is not mine. I ran cattle for years over land on which you men are located. It was not my land. It was government land. It is your land now. You have homesteaded it."

"Then you want peace?" a man asked.

"I do not want trouble."

Cal watched his farmers. He guessed that this talk had cost Paul Malone a lot. It took guts to stand up before your enemies and ask for peace. He flashed a look at Eddie, but the girl was watching the expressions of the hoemen. He wished she would look his way, but she didn't.

Cal found himself studying the firm small jaw, the long slope of her cheek, the tilt of her nose, the lips open with excitement. Then she turned and looked at him. She caught him in his mood, but her face did not soften. Instead he thought it hardened, and he looked away.

Farmers asked questions. Gates had been left open. Heart Circle and Bar N cattle had grazed in wheat-fields. Malone had only one answer: he had not ordered fences cut or pulled down or that gates be opened and dropped.

"Then Pete Glenn is our only enemy?"

"As far as I'm concerned, he is—if you want to look upon him as trouble. I don't know his plans. That is between him an' you. Your biggest enemy is goin' to be drought, I think."

Cal said, "Thanks, Mr. Malone."

Malone and Eddie walked to the door while Cal dismissed the farmers. They crowded around the Heart Circle pair and asked questions. Cal said, "Well, did it settle anything, Hutchinson?"

Jack Hutchinson scowled. "I believe we did, Cal. When Malone came along he helped us out a lot. That was good of him."

The farmers were still talking to Paul Malone. Eddie had pulled out of the group and stood alone to one side.

Cal said, "May I take you to your horse, Miss Eddie?"

"Thank you."

She and her father had tied their broncs in the brush. Cal took her elbow, for in the dark the footing was uncertain. He liked the feel of her firm arm. Once she stumbled.

"Be careful."

He untied her horse. She stood beside her animal, watching him. A bird made night-

149

sounds in the timber. Both were silent for some time.

"Those farmers—I hope we get rain. They have children and wives. Cal—"

"Yes?"

"Oh, nothing."

Cal put his arm around her. He had expected her to draw back, but she didn't. Instead, she was laughing quietly.

"Cal, I've played hard to get. Cal, I've—"

"Don't talk any more."

There were a million thoughts in him, and the night had taken on a million hues of brightness. She pressed against him, firm and pleasing, and her lips were moist. Then an explosion rocked the range.

The roar broke into them, jerking them apart. Somewhere something flared, washing the range with the light of lightning. Then the explosion died.

"What was that?"

Cal said, "Somebody blew up my granary!"

13

THE man who called himself John Shane had left Puma City about the same time Jack Hutchinson and Cal Rutherford had ridden out to warn the nesters. The man known as John Shane had added this all together and had figured out where Pete Glenn and Marfa Jordan would soon hit.

Still, he was not sure. You can put yourself in the other man's Justins and try to think from his viewpoint, but still you're not he, you're still yourself and therefore liable to error. John Shane knew this. Therefore he played his cards close. He had gambled with death on other jobs. Here he was, gambling with lead cards . . . again.

This thought pulled a smile to his dark lips. He was certain this would lead to guns. In his way of thinking, based upon the circumstances he had seen and met, he saw no other ending. His was a calling that demanded night-rides and a close mouth. He had utilized both during his brief stay in Puma Valley.

He added up events in his mind, piling them as a child piles his blocks, placing them in chronological order. Now, riding out of town, he studied these blocks, trying accurately to judge the relationship one to the other. Cal Rutherford was Pete Glenn's enemy.

They were not enemies through personal hatred. Theirs was not an enmity sired by physical dislike. They were enemies because their goals conflicted and clashed. Glenn wanted Puma Valley for his cattle. Cal Rutherford wanted Puma Valley for his farmers.

Therefore Glenn and Rutherford were enemies.

That was the first block: the fundamental block. On it all other blocks rested their weight. The second block represented the drought. That was beyond the ken and aid of man and therefore John Shane did not reckon with it. The third block represented the wheat-tanker going over the cliff.

John Shane had made a mistake in reckoning that night. He had come too late, and the deed was over with. He had ridden along the road in the dark and had thought the tanker had made town. Instead, it had lain broken in the gully below. Broken, with Jimmy Stephens unconscious beside it.

Yes, he had erred there.

He knew that Pete Glenn had sicked Marfa Jordan on Cal Rutherford. Glenn had given Jordan orders to kill Rutherford there on Puma City's main-stem. But Rutherford had not packed a gun and it had gone into fists. And Rutherford had whipped Marfa Jordan. Jordan, who had expected to kill Rutherford with his huge, terrible hands.

That outcome had upset Pete Glenn's timetable.

For John Shane knew the principles of Glenn's warfare. At first Glenn had played cards under the table to get the nesters to break with Cal Rutherford. But Rutherford's hold on the hoemen had been too strong. That part of Glenn's reckoning had fallen far short of promise and purpose.

Glenn had accordingly forsaken that campaign and had placed it in another man's hands—a man as greedy as the Bar N owner. John Shane knew who this man was but he was waiting. The time was not ripe.

Riding through the heat, the man who called himself a gambler let his thoughts still pick their way. Glenn and Malone had broken because Malone favored peace, not war. That had made little difference to Pete Glenn, though.

Glenn had then put Marfa Jordan against Jack Jones. That move had not been directed because of hate toward Jones. No personal antipathy had been involved. But with Jones dead—killed by the Bar N gunman—the farmers might flare up into open gun-war.

And Pete Glenn wanted gun-war. He had killers on his payroll. He wanted the hoemen to move against him. For if the farmers made the first move, the Bar N would then be clear in the eyes of local people—hadn't the sodbusters moved against the Bar N? And Glenn wanted that.

So Jones had died for a purpose, and that purpose had failed. For Cal Rutherford would hold the farmers intact and under his command. John Shane was already figuring on Glenn's move to fall short.

For Glenn had used the wrong thinking. He wasn't counting enough on the wives and kids or the farmers. John Shane had stood in the Mercantile and on the streets and he had heard those wives talking among themselves. And the consensus was this: before they let their men ride to war against the Bar N or Heart Circle, they would demand their men leave the country.

There was no fight in these nester women. This land had turned against them, it had become powder under their heels, and without rain it had no future or promise—it could not build new homes and barns and educate and feed children. They would not fight for something of no value.

And in that respect, John Shane had reasoned, men differed from women. Men fought not for monetary or property gain; they fought for an elusive thing called honor. And honor was close kin to pride. And Pete Glenn was proud.

This would be the flaw in Glenn's make-up.

So far, Cal Rutherford had outwitted Pete Glenn. Rutherford had turned the tables against Marfa Jordan, and an affront against Jordan was victory against Pete Glenn. Glenn's pride demanded he hit in retaliation. So far, this pride had been submerged beneath cunningness.

But another upset, and Glenn's pride would break through, forcing him into open action.

And that action would take the part of gunsmoke.

When that pride became too great, Pete Glenn would move in to kill Cal Rutherford openly.

John Shane thought, That time is close. A man can feel it in the air, along with this heat.

He had his plans drawn. He would wait for that moment when Rutherford and Glenn openly clashed. Then he would come out with what he knew and what he had seen, and this thing would be over. There was danger—raw, terrible danger—in it; he knew this—he was definitely aware of this danger. But danger had ridden by his stirrup, moving with his horse, for many years.

He sighed. Too many years . . .

He pulled his bronc into the buck-brush of a small knoll. Here he and horse were hidden; he took his field-glasses, untying them from his saddle. He settled beside a rock and watched and waited.

Yonder, far away, he saw two riders—these, he found out later, were Cal Rutherford and Jack Hutchinson, riding out to get the hoemen to the schoolhouse. He watched them and found their identities. For some moments he kept the glasses on them, and then he swept the lenses across the basin, looking for something he did not expect to find, and he did not find it.

He lowered the glasses. He did not use them much again, except occasionally to check on the progress of Rutherford and Hutchinson. The afternoon tiptoed by on hot, uncertain feet. The sun slid down and twilight came and with it came Pete Glenn and Marfa Jordan.

They rode toward the Bar N, not more than one hundred yards away. John Shane wished he knew the nature of their conversation. He did not follow them. There was no percentage in that.

Glenn and Jordan went toward the Bar N John Shane watched the farmers leave their homes and drive rigs toward the schoolhouse. By this time it was so dark, the field glasses were useless against the encroaching night.

He thought, Where will Glenn and Jordan hit next?

The wives and kids of the farmers would be out with rifles. This trouble had come down to that. He doubted seriously if the Bar N men would move further against the farmers. Glenn would let the murder of Jack Jones rest on the hoemen and knock their nerves and patiences raw and fretful.

The elevator?

John Shane shook his head. Glenn wanted that elevator for himself. The last thing he would do would be burn that elevator. But the man would still commit a nuisance raid. Shane was sure of that.

The granary?

Shane leaned back, eyes closed. He sat that way for an hour. Then he went to his bronc, put his field-glasses in their case, tightened his cinch and went up. He rode toward Cal Rutherford's granary.

He was tired. This night work was tiresome and days were too hot for sleeping. His head came down and he dozed. But it was not a sound sleep. He had trained himself to doze, and yet any little noise—anything alien—would quickly bring him awake. He rode and came to the brush in the creek below the granary.

He came in with a great vigilance, and because of long practice he moved silently. He left his bronc and settled with his rifle. He knew Ed Stuart's boy guarded the granary. He knew that the boy stayed across the clearing on that small crest of hills crowned by the black rocks. The boy would be there now, probably asleep.

Twice before John Shane had crept up on the Stuart boy and found him asleep. He had not awakened him. He had stepped back carefully, building his trail back, and he had watched the granary. He hardly blamed the boy for sleeping on the job. Days were too hot for a day-sleeper.

So John Shane waited, and John Shane dozed. And around midnight he heard the rider come in. He heard the horse stop, and he heard the man dismount. The night was dark and John Shane waited.

Had Cal Rutherford ridden over from the schoolhouse to check the granary-guard before heading into Puma City? John Shane stood up, rifle in hand. He could see nobody, hear nobody. Evidently the Stuart boy still slept.

Then he saw the flare. It made a fine, high arc, with fire spilling quietly behind it. Dynamite! It landed beside the granary. John Shane heard a man run; John Shane fired.

He was running ahead, aiming to get out of danger, for the powder would blast soon, he knew. He figured the Stuart boy would be out of danger, for the rocks would shelter him and he was quite a distance from the granary.

And as he ran, he fired. He made his Winchester talk a steady flame that blossomed like a red wild rose. He heard the return fire. The bullet sang, a dim hornet-like sound; then the cartridge cracked. He had little chance to hit anything. The night was dark; his target uncertain. He glimpsed a man, lost him. His rifle was empty. He went to one knee.

A piece of board hit the brush behind him. That was the last of the falling debris from the granary. The explosion had lifted the frame granary, and wheat had mushroomed up and had fallen like rice. John Shane dug into his pocket and came out with cartridges.

"Who's out there?"

A scared voice, squeaky through fear and adolescence. It brought a smile to John Shane. Up ahead a horse was breaking brush. The Stuart boy shot at the sound. The horse kept on running and John Shane listened. But the stride was even and therefore the bronc was unwounded.

"I got to get out of here."

The man known as John Shane found his horse, crammed his rifle into boot, and rode away, riding slowly. He kept the horse on the edge of a ploughed field and therefore it made no noise. The night had become still again. Already the roar of the dynamite had lost itself in the silent folds of darkness. Already the sounds of the powderman's retreating bronc were lost.

Now, out of hearing distance, John Shane fed his horse rowels. He cut the trail angling toward the Bar N and drew in here. He waited for a few minutes. But if a rider had passed this way, he had already ridden past this point. And John Shane realized he had missed again.

They do things fast on this range, he thought.

He sat his horse there for some time. Now, somewhere in the night, riders swept ahead, riding for the granary. That would be Cal Rutherford and the farmers from the meeting. They had heard the explosion.

John Shane sat his bronc, waiting, watching, listening. The riders went by and he heard the dull retreat of their broncs' hoofs. He stirred in saddle and sent his bronc toward Puma City.

The night-ride had netted nothing. He had been outwitted and it had happened too fast. He had not been able to identify the man who had dynamited the granary. He came into town, horse at a walk. He met nobody and nobody passed him on the road. Evidently Cal Rutherford was still back at the granary.

At the edge of Puma City, he drew rein and looked out across the valley. There were no lights. The range was dark; his thoughts were dark. He left his bronc in the livery stable. The old hostler was in bed and John Shane unsaddled his bronc and rubbed him down with an old gunny-sack.

He worked methodically, doubling the sack many times, making a compact object of it. The grain of the sack was coarse on his hands. He rubbed the horse, working out the dust, sucking up the sweat. Sweat came on his own forehead. Still he kept on rubbing; one sack got too wet and dirty—he got another.

Glenn had taken another bite into his problem. John Shane analyzed it as he worked; only two conclusions could be attained. Glenn would either hit next at the elevator or at Cal Rutherford.

Rutherford's wheat was gone. What little money he could have got from its sale was now a thing to be remembered but money never to be touched. The dynamite had scattered wheat over dozens of acres.

He doubted if Glenn would try to destroy the

elevator. The elevator cost money, and when Glenn controlled this valley it would be useful to him. Also, from here on out Rutherford and his farmers would double-guard the high building.

John Shane finished his job. He was standing beside the hotel when Cal Rutherford came along the sidewalk, boot-heels loud in the night against the plank walk. Shane moved forward.

Rutherford stopped. They were the only two men on the street, and the hour was late and John Shane caught the sharp edge of Cal Rutherford's suspicion.

"John Shane."

"Cal Rutherford."

Shane stopped. "You're up late, Rutherford. I recall hearing you and your farmers met tonight. The meeting ran on late."

"It did."

Shane waited, wanting to know something, yet not daring to ask. He was a poker-player. He didn't want to tip his hand.

"Nice night. Still hot."

"Always hot. You're up late, Shane."

"Only time it's a little cool." Shane looked at the stars. He seemed busy with them. "I heard an explosion about two hours ago. I wonder if a meteor fell out on the range?"

"Dynamite, not a meteor."

Shane said, "Dynamite?"

Rutherford spoke quietly. "Somebody blasted my granary sky high. Destroyed all my wheat. Young Stuart was on guard. He got in a few shots."

"Hit anybody?"

"No bodies around."

"Oh."

Rutherford said, "Funny thing, though. Stuart tells me before he got into the shootin' scrape he saw two rifles makin' flares. Two men were shootin' at each other."

"Who would that be?"

"I don't know. Unless somebody aimed to kill the Glenn man who slung the dynamite. The kid went to sleep on the job. But who would be out to sling lead into a Glenn man, at that hour of the night?"

"Maybe Jimmy?"

"I doubt it. I gave him orders to stay at the elevator. He follows them most of the time."

"Maybe a Glenn man didn't dynamite it. Maybe Paul Malone was behind it."

"Malone was at the meeting."

John Shane yawned. "Me for my soogans."

Cal Rutherford went toward his elevator. Shane looked at the black bulk of it spearing its height into the night. He stood in the darkness of the doorway and watched Rutherford. *The end of this is ahead,* he thought.

14

THE man spurred his black gelding out of the brush. He hollered, "Hello, there," and the oncoming rider pulled in, bronc rearing against the cruelty of a spade-bit. "How'd it turn out, Marfa?"

Marfa Jordan let his reins go slack. The bronc settled down, the pressure leaving the bit. Jordan said, "I got one, Pete. Through the left shoulder. A rifle ball, out of the dark—Just luck—"

Pete Glenn's voice showed his surprise. "You got shot?"

"Not much. In the shoulder."

Glenn swung his bronc around. "We'd best ride to the house, Marfa. But who the devil winged you? We've scouted that granary. Each night that Stuart kid goes to sleep within a few minutes after goin' on the job. You must've made too much noise an' woke him up.

Jordan spilled his story in terse words. No, he hadn't awakened the Stuart boy. He'd come in through the dark, flung his dynamite, and ridden out. And the kid had been asleep in the rocks.

"Then the kid never shot you? Is that it, Jordan?"

They were in the Bar N ranch-house now. Pete Glenn lit a lamp, hand trembling a little; Jordan sat down on a straight-back chair. The lamplight showed blood on Marfa Jordan's left shoulder.

"Good luck it was my left shoulder," Jordan grunted.

Glenn repeated, "Was it the kid who shot you?"

Jordan shook his head. "They was somebody else cached in the brush. The kid got in some shots after that powder popped. But somebody else shot me from the brush. Now who the devil would it be?"

Pete Glenn stood, plainly thinking. "I sure don't know, Marfa. It weren't Cal Rutherford. He was at the meeting." Glenn talked as he cut off Marfa Jordan's shirt, knife glistening in the lamplight. The knife was as sharp as a razor. It made a small murmur as it parted the heavy woollen cloth.

For Pete Glenn had watched the schoolhouse wherein Cal Rutherford and the farmers had met. From the hill behind the school, he had kept watch; there in the rocks he had hidden. And he had seen Paul and Eddie Malone ride over from the Heart Circle.

"They went inside, Marfa."

By this time, Marfa Jordan's left shoulder was bare. Blood had dried on it. The wound lay ugly and dirty, looking up at Pete Glenn. Glenn's fingers probed and pushed and once or twice Marfa Jordan winced.

"I don't know how it did it," Pete Glenn finally said. "It must've been a steel-jacketed cartridge. It went under your collar-bone, between the bone and the high rib, and tore out some flesh. No bones busted."

"Should I see Doc Wilson?"

Pete Glenn's face was bleak. "Not unless we have to. Doc is a great gab-hound; he tells all he knows and what he imagines. We'll see how you feel come mornin'. You'd best hit the soogans."

"My money?"

Pete Glenn opened a drawer on the sideboard and tossed Marfa Jordan a small roll of bills which Jordan caught in his right hand. The gunman looked at the money, a sour smile on his whiskery lips.

"And for this, I get shot through the shoulder. . . ."

Glenn snapped, "There's more ahead!" He was raw and irritable. Who had shot Jordan? Maybe Jordan was wrong. Maybe the Stuart kid had shot him, at that. On a dark night—with confusion and dynamite—

"There was another man there," Jordan repeated.

Glenn said, "Get to bed, fellow."

Jordan got to his feet, moving with the stiffness of a saddleman on boots. Glenn stood and listened to the clomp-clomp of Jordan's boots as he went down the hall. Glenn heard a door open, heard it close, heard a window creak as it went up. The wind came in the open door, and it held a touch of night's coldness.

The Bar N owner felt this coolness, and it registered against him, bringing the thought that maybe rain was in the distance. This thought brought him across the porch and sent his gaze up at the sky. Not a cloud. Only the stars. Dawn was not far away. This night had seen much.

Just what had it seen? What had been done?

The meeting, for one thing. Paul Malone had lined up with the nesters. Pete Glenn was sure

169

of that. Otherwise, Malone and his daughter would not have ridden in and gone into the schoolhouse. That left the Bar N alone to buck the nesters. Was that good . . . or bad?

Glenn moved back on the porch. He stood there and looked over his buildings. He had immense pride in his ranch . . . and in himself. He was, in a measure, glad to see Malone riding the middle-rail of neutrality. Malone had been no use to him, anyway. Malone had only been a convenient person on whom to dump wrong-doings done by the Bar N. Malone could still lie used in that capacity.

And would the farmers really believe Paul Malone did not want to fight them? Pete Glenn smiled at that thought. These farmers were suspicious; their lives, the lives of their families, demanded they be suspicious.

He could not see where Paul Malone had bettered the lot of the Heart Circle, nor could he see that the Bar N had lost anything.

So much for that.

With the granary demolished, with the wheat destroyed—now Cal Rutherford had no way to get any money. Yesterday he could have hauled in his wheat and shipped it east and drawn money. Now the wheat was scattered from hell to tincup. Cal Rutherford was broke now.

A touch of doubt began to burn in Pete Glenn's mind. Marfa Jordan had left in a hurry. He had not stayed behind to check the damage done by his powder. Maybe the wheat had not been blown up? Pete Glenn walked the floor, hands behind him. His thoughts were solidified.

He heard a rider come into the yard. One stride, he cupped his hand over the chimney— and the lamp was blown out. He went to the doorway and crossed the blackness of the porch. He waited there. The horse stopped and Pete Glenn could see his dim outlines. He saw the outline of a man leaving the saddle.

"Howdy, the house."

Glenn felt tension seep out of him. "Come in Hutchinson."

"I've got but a few minutes." Hutchinson crossed the porch, leaving his horse sod-tied. "I rode fast to get out here. I got to get back before dark. You blew that wheat sky high. Good work. It's a total loss."

"I feel better now," Glenn said, grinning.

Hutchinson said, "Jordan get wounded?"

Glenn looked at the railroad superintendent. Inside there was a cold hand that clenched and unclenched. Marfa Jordan hadn't mentioned talking with Jack Hutchinson. Then how did Hutchinson know about Jordan's wound?

"Explain yourself."

Jack Hutchinson looked at him. Glenn knew the railroad man was trying to probe through the question for meaning. Hutchinson could not find his answer, so he shrugged.

"A farmer got a lantern. We looked around. I saw the spot first, but before I could kick dirt over it, Cal Rutherford saw it."

"Blood?"

"Yes, blood."

Glenn told about Marfa Jordan's wound. He told about the third man coming in—the man who had shot Jordan. "Now who the devil was he?"

Hutchinson stood silent, face showing thought. He let his mind go methodically across the basin, checking farm after farm. Finally he said, "All the farmers were there. Every man jack of them. So no farmer was around that granary. But it might be one of the farmer's boys were over there."

"The Stuart kid mention another kid with him on guard?"

Hutchinson shook his head. "He said he was alone."

Glenn clenched and opened his palms. He looked at his clean hands. "Then that angle is out. Hutchinson, there's somebody else—somebody we don't know—in on this. There must be."

Hutchinson shook his head. "Who would it be?" He answered his own question. "Nobody." He walked to the window. "We've played close cards. Nobody knows you and I are workin' together. Tonight softened the farmers toward me. They'd swear I was out to help them."

He turned, smile enigmatic.

"We're sittin' pretty, Glenn. Only one thing is wrong. You got to keep Marfa Jordan in hiding."

"Why?"

"Why ask?"

Glenn said, "I asked *why*?"

Anger touched Jack Hutchinson's cheeks. The railroad superintendent brushed his small mustache and watched Pete Glenn.

"Glenn, that's a foolish question. What if Cal Rutherford or some farmer finds out Marfa Jordan has a bullet wound in his shoulder like

173

you tell me? They'll know then he's the gent who got shot at that explosion."

"What about it?"

"What about it?" Hutchinson repeated the question with surprise. "That'll be a blueprint pointin' to you as instigator behind that explosion. Those farmers'll move against the Bar N."

"I know that."

Jack Hutchinson's eyelids came down, blue and thin in the lamplight. "I guess I don't follow you, Pete. I guess once again you're a jump ahead of me."

"Two jumps, anyway."

Hutchinson snarled, "All right, tell me!"

The railroad man had overstepped. He was instantly aware of that. For Pete Glenn stopped walking. He stood and he looked at Hutchinson, and there was wild hell in the eyes of Pete Glenn.

"Don't snap at me, you fox-terrier! You don't boss me, savvy. You're operatin' on Pete Glenn's money, an' don't forget it at any time."

Hutchinson's face was the color of a dirty blanket. He raised his hand and rubbed his thin mustache. Glenn noticed the tremble in the well-kept fingers. He noticed this and it drove anger out of him.

"Sorry, Jack."

Hutchinson said, "I rubbed you. Then you aim to kill Cal Rutherford? Is that your next move, Pete?"

"Cal Rutherford has to go, Hutchinson."

Jack Hutchinson took that into his mind. He rolled it and held it up and looked at it and pondered on it. And Pete Glenn watched the railroad superintendent. Watched, and wondered at Hutchinson's true thoughts.

But one man cannot see into another man's brain. They were bound into this by invisible ropes. Ropes both could feel but could not see.

Hutchinson said, "He dies."

Hutchinson left.

By night infection had set into the wound on Marfa Jordan's shoulder. The gunman spent a sick night. Glenn said, "We'd best get you into town, Jordan."

"Doc Wilson will tell Cal Rutherford."

Glenn said, "Maybe that would be best."

Jordan looked at his boss. Jordan's eyes were flushed. He moved his right hand, bringing it up, bending the elbow, his gun jumping from leather.

"I can still shoot fast with my right hand."

15

CAL RUTHERFORD woke to an afternoon of intense heat that seemed to cling to the walls of his room in the elevator. He awoke wet with sweat. He lay there and grouped his thoughts. The memory of the night came back—the meeting at the schoolhouse, the dynamiting of his wheat.

The blinds were down and the room was semi-dark. He heard boots outside, and Jimmy Stephens looked in.

"You awake, Cal?"

"No, I'm still asleep."

"You talk good in your sleep." Jimmy came inside, limping a little. "There's a coupla farmers outside who want to blab with you."

"What about?"

"This elevator."

Cal remembered. He sat on the edge of the bed and felt for his boots. "We're puttin' a two-man guard around this property every night from here on in, Jimmy. They prob'ly come in for tonight's guard."

177

Jimmy nodded. "Make it easier on me, Cal. I'd like to find out who slugged me an' wrecked that grain-wagon."

"Forget it, kid."

"Pete Glenn," Jimmy said. "Glenn an' Marfa Jordan."

Cal said quickly, "Don't talk that way around anybody but me. Let Jordan catch word of what you just told me an' you might turn up dead. These boys are playin' for keeps. That dynamite last night proved that."

Cal dressed. He was dog-tired. The hot days and nights, the worry, the lack of sleep—this everpresent trouble. He talked with the two farmers who turned out to be Ev Minter and Pop Atherton. They would stand the first half of the guard and Jimmy and Cal would stand from midnight to daylight.

This settled, Cal went downtown. John Shane sat in the rocker on the porch of the hotel. Cal stopped and leaned against the pillar. Shane rocked, silent, watching the town, watching Cal. Cal got the swift impression that somewhere this man fitted. He was part of this puzzle. But where did John Shane fit in?

Or did he fit in?

There was this riddle, and other riddles.

Shane said, "Hot again."

Cal said, "Some day it'll end. It has to end." This conversation had no real purpose. It covered something with its irrelevancy. But what did it cover?

"I was down to the depot at noon," Shane said slowly. "The operator told me it was raining over in Saco. That's a hundred miles away. But it might reach here. Let's hope so."

Cal felt a wild thrust of hope.

John Shane was silent. Cal noticed that from his vantage point this man could watch Doc Wilson's office. Shane was looking at the sign: J. M. Wilson, M.D. He was looking at it with vacant eyes.

"There was blood?" Shane asked.

"I don't follow you."

Shane looked up at Cal. "Out by the granary," he supplied.

"How did you know?"

Shane shrugged. "I heard, I guess. A farmer. I forget where I got that information." He was noncommittal. He was uninterested.

"He got wounded," Cal said.

Shane nodded, his mind apparently on other matters. Cal got the impression the man wanted to be alone. He walked down the plank walk

179

and thought, He's a funny bird. I can't place him here. Then he dismissed this with, I reckon he's just a gambler, but he does show up in odd places at odd times. He turned into Doc Wilson's office.

The medico was asleep with his gross body crammed into his swivel-chair, thick head on his thick chest, his lips moving with each breath. Cal sat down and looked at the man and then the doctor opened his eyes. He raised his head. He was shaggy and keen and smart.

"Well, Cal?"

Cal said, "A bullet found that man who dynamited that granary. I was wondering if he'd been to you for treatment."

The eyes watched him.

"Has he?"

"I don't know."

Cal got to his feet, smiling slightly. "In other words, you won't tell me, huh? Is that it?"

"I took an oath." Doc Wilson gestured toward the printing framed on the wall. "My duty is to heal. Be he killer or saint, that's my sworn duty, Cal."

"Sorry," Cal said.

The elevator-man walked outside. He went past the hotel, and John Shane still sat there, and Cal turned and asked, "Did anybody go into the doc's office this morning so far?"

"Would I know?"

"You watch that office."

Shane allowed himself a smile. Cal watched it grow and marvelled at its coldness. "You have eyes, Rutherford." Shane sighed quietly. "Nobody had gone in there yet."

"What's this trouble to you, Shane?"

The question was blunt. But Cal Rutherford was in a blunt mood. He wanted this over with. He wanted this matter sealed and solved and delivered. He had been hitting here, striking here, moving ahead, coming back, sallying and trying to find this enemy.

Not that he didn't know the identities of his enemies. They were, he knew, Pete Glenn and Marfa Jordan. But so far he had not caught either in a wrong. So far he had battered his head against a stone wall.

Shane watched him. He seemed to be weighing him. Then Shane said, "Nothing, Rutherford, nothing."

This answer did not please Cal Rutherford. Maybe Shane saw this displeasure in the elevator-man's eyes, read it in the facial expression. For Shane went blank and dead and limp and silent.

Cal said, "Just thought I'd ask."

"No harm."

Jack Hutchinson came out of the Merc. "Raining this side of Saco, Cal. They say it's coming this way. Hope it makes it."

"Long ways," Cal said.

Hutchinson said, "It would save most of the crops, Cal. Those farmers of yours could haul in grain to your elevator this fall. One rain would head that grain out and make a crop."

"They wouldn't sell out to you then." This hope was wild. Maybe the rain would not come this far. "A rain would wreck your plans, Hutchinson."

Hutchinson shrugged. "I reckon so." He seemed unconcerned. Cal figured this was just a pose. This man was another part of this riddle. This whole range was involved in this riddle.

"I've bought quite a bit of land," Hutchinson reminded him.

The railroad-superintendent went to the depot. Cal leaned against the bank, enjoying the shade, watching Doc Wilson's office. So far he had met nothing but rebuffs. He went to his elevator. Jimmy Stephens was whittling in the shade. Cal squatted beside him.

He asked Jimmy to station himself on the hotel porch and watch Doc Wilson's office.

"Why?"

"That gent with the dynamite last night, kid. He stopped a bullet. He might need medical treatment."

"Okay, Cal."

Cal Rutherford went to the barn and got his bronc. He lifted his Miles City kak and placed it on the saddle-blanket and rode out of town. He headed for the blasted granary.

Many thoughts rode in the saddle with him. It was good to be out in the open range with a horse moving under your legs. He let the pony lope but the heat was too much; the bronc settled into a fast walk.

He found a trail, followed it; he left this trail, cutting across country until he reached the wagon-road. He circled the granary, looking for tracks. He saw tracks and he went down and looked at them. But this plan would turn out purposeless; he had almost accepted that from the start.

For one thing, many animals travelled these fenced lanes, and therefore the loose dust was marked by many hoofs. He found no tracks that looked substantial, and he turned back toward town. The wind came from the west and it had a touch of coolness that was drying the sweat and dust on his bronc.

He thought, "Maybe the rain will reach this far." That thought was good because rain is good. A rider angled in. Eddie Malone rode her pinto. The sunlight was glistening on the bronze of her hair and she was slender in her saddle.

"I saw you over by the granary, Cal. You were looking for tracks?"

"I was lookin' for a needle in a haystack."

"Too many riders had been around," she said. The pinto fell into pace beside Cal's horse. They made a pretty picture: this girl with the golden wild hair, this pinto splashed with gaudy colors. Cal glanced at her, not wanting to look boldly, not wanting to be too open in his gaze.

"Too many riders," she repeated.

Cal said, "You said that before." He was slightly jumpy, and he kept thinking of their meeting outside the schoolhouse. That was the only bright spot on this range. She was the bright spot. Without Eddie, this would be a lifeless fight—a fight without emotion and for material things only. Warmth came in and pushed away his nervousness.

"Cal."

"Yes."

"Pete Glenn and Marfa Jordan—" She paused. She looked at her horizon. "Well, this is hard to say, Cal."

He waited, knowing what she was going to say.

She kept on watching the horizon and its rimrock and hills. Then she looked at him, and she had a touch of tears. "Cal, they're out to kill you! You know that, and I know it, and the whole range knows it."

Cal nodded. "That's foreseen." He added, "it's been in that class for a long, long time now. You're thinkin' of last night, Eddie?"

"How could I forget it?"

Her words made him happy and his face showed it. He did not put his horse close to put his arm around her. She had found him, and he was her man; now fear was quick in her, acid in sharpness—fear that she would lose him. That made it harder for him, too. Much harder.

"There are two of them, Cal."

He had thought of that, too. He had taken

185

full cognizance of his danger. For months he had mulled it over. Always it had been with him—a darkness upon the rimrock, the shadows under the cottonwoods. Two of them. Pete Glenn, dandified, quick as a shadow, deadly as he was fascinating. And Marfa Jordan, shuffling, huge, with the dull animal intelligence, the animal eyes, and reflexes attuned to reaching for a six-shooter. . . .

"Maybe they both won't jump me at once."

She said, violent with hate, "You should have killed Jordan. Too bad you never had a gun on you. Too bad you had to use your fists on him that day!"

This was a new facet to her character, an aspect had not seen before. And he said, "Listen, Eddie, this is my fight. Be it two of them or one, I can't and won't run. I've got Jimmy for one. He can shoot and shoot straight. And who knows if it will end in six-guns? Maybe we're both a little upset."

She shook her head.

They did not ride fast. They did not speak often. Most of the ride was made in silence except for the clop-clop of a bronc's hoofs in the dust. The west wind still held a chill.

Maybe the rain would come. Maybe it would not come.

There were two mysteries then on this grass —the trouble and this rain that would not fall. But a man could do something with the trouble. He could meet it and down it or it could down him. The trouble could be settled.

And then, to Cal Rutherford, it became clear. Up to now the lines had shifted, it had been mirage-like; now it was cold and clear and every detail was plain. The whole thing crystallized and became certain.

He would move against the Bar N men. Take them one at a time, and either run them out of this Puma Valley country . . . or kill them. That was, after all, the only solution. There was no other way out.

Up to now he had known uncertainty. Maybe the blasting of the granary had unconsciously cemented his purpose. He did not know. He did not care. But one thing was certain—it stood out like a peak among hills—and this certainty was that the next time he met Pete Glenn or Marfa Jordan he would call their gun.

Suddenly he felt better.

He glanced at Eddie. She had a rifle stuck in

her saddleboot. He had not asked her why she rode for Puma City. He knew.

She had worried about him. She had given in to him at last, admitting her own stubbornness. She had deliberately held her thoughts away from him because he was with the nesters and her father was a big cowman.

The way for her had not been too easy. He was aware of this for the first time, and it had little warmth. She had no call to tote a rifle on her saddle. He had never seen her carry a rifle before.

So she had ridden in, wondering if he were still alive, and if he were alive if he would need help. He liked that thought and yet he disliked it, for he did not want a woman entangled in this violence. But he said nothing.

And so they came to Puma City.

16

JIMMY STEPHENS was panting. Jimmy Stephens said, "Cal, they came! They went in the back door of Doc Wilson's office! I seen them, Cal!"

"Who?"

"Pete Glenn an' Marfa Jordan! They come in the back so's nobody'd see them. Glenn an' Jordan! An' Jordan didn't walk so good."

"His leg?"

"No, his legs looked all right. But it looked like his left shoulder was bandaged. Anyway, there was a bulge under his shirt."

"How long ago?"

"About five minutes, I'd say. I run to the elevator lookin' for you, then come here to the barn." The youth carried a rifle. He caught his breath, cheeks bright from running. "You come into town just in time."

Cal stood in the doorway of the barn and looked at Eddie Malone, who was about a block away, heading for the business section. He was suddenly glad Eddie had not been around to hear Jimmy's story.

For the girl would have been excited. And Cal Rutherford did not want her actively tied up in this oncoming trouble. For that matter, he himself had little taste or desire for it. He forced himself to accept it with a calmness that surprised even himself.

"You sure Jordan is wounded?"

"He must be. That looked like a bandage under his shirt. He didn't walk too steady. An' why did they go in the back?"

Cal nodded. The kid was undoubtedly right. He looked at Jimmy's rifle. "What do you aim to do with that?"

The harshness of the boy's voice was revealing of the unrest inside. "They's two of them, Cal. You took me off'n a freight an' gave me the only home I've ever knew. There's only you. Not a farmer in town when you need them. So I'm sidin' you, friend, whether you like it or not."

Cal smiled tightly. "You give me little choice."

"They shoved me over that cliff, not you. I was lucky to get outa that wreck alive. You owe them hate, Cal. I admit that. But I owe them hate, too. Your fight is my fight."

"You might get killed."

"By heavens, they'll kill me before they kill you."

Cal had always known the youth had cottoned to him strongly. But he had never guessed the boy liked him so much. The thought brought a strange tightness to him, and he put his hand on Jimmy's shoulder.

"Jimmy, neither of us will get killed. You can bet on that. With you an' me both buckin' the same tigers, we'll come out winners sure as shootin'."

"Damn' right we'll win, Cal."

Cal was only talking to cheer himself up and to cheer Jimmy. A bullet, he realized, didn't care whom it killed. He was going into this with misgivings. Had there been any law, or a law officer, in Puma City, he would have turned the matter over to him, swearing out a warrant charging Marfa Jordan with dynamiting the granary.

Still, he had practically no evidence against Jordan or Glenn. Just because Jordan had a bum shoulder was no sign he had been shot. Maybe a horse had thrown him. . . . A thousand doubts assailed Cal Rutherford. Maybe Jordan and Glenn would not fight even if he and Jimmy called the Bar N pair?

He realized he was thinking wrong on that last point. Jordan and Glenn had to have him out of the way in order to gain control of Puma Valley. With him dead, the farmers would troop out . . . rain or no rain. Fear would be on them and fear would drive them off their land.

So, evidence or no evidence, this trouble was here. It stared Cal Rutherford in the face with a direct gaze.

"Come on, Jimmy."

They went toward the downtown business district. Jimmy fell in beside Cal, and Cal noticed the youth still limped slightly from his fall down the canyon. Cal also knew the fall had injured Jimmy Stephen's pride as much as it had done physical injury to his hip.

He played with this idea. He had been similar to Jimmy when he had been sixteen. He too had had a hot temper. Only by effort—sheer willpower and physical effort—had he learned to control his temper. He had worked with Jimmy, telling him someday his violent temper would get him into serious trouble.

And the youth had responded. In the months

they had been together, Jimmy had matured a lot. Cal had seen to it he got plenty of responsibilities. For he knew that responsibility matured a man and gave him purpose and character.

Jimmy was proud. Now his pride had been rubbed with coarse sand-paper. They had jumped him from behind, wrecked the grain-wagon, thrown him unconscious into that canyon. Only by a miracle had he pulled through. But he would never forget that assault.

Cal thought, I'd've been just as anxious as he is when I was sixteen. This was a warm thought. It fitted in. Jimmy was a man despite his adolescent years. He'd bummed and worked and fought his way through life. Only an accident had taken him to Puma City.

Cal was glad this accident had occurred. He thought a lot of the kid; now the boy, in his blunt way, was repaying him. Still, the idea persisted—it played through his brain, cutting corners. What if the kid got hurt? Or killed?

That thought was terrible. It was as if a piece of ice had been laid around his heart to freeze it and strangle him. Cal wished, then, the youth had not blundered onto this. But he had and that was that. A man couldn't argue with fate or circumstance.

He had to accept them . . . and let it go at that. That was one of the first lessons a man learned when he shifted for himself.

Jimmy would want it no other way. Cal was sure of that—sure of it as he was sure of himself. The youth would ask one thing—and that to side Cal Rutherford. He would ask nothing more.

They came into an alley, and Cal fell back a pace. For a moment a wild thought smashed across him, and he almost drew his .45 from holster. Jimmy's back was toward him; he could raise the gun quickly; he could bring it down across the boy's skull. The boy would unspring at the knees. By the time he came to, this trouble would be over. And Jimmy would be safe.

But logic held that move. If he did that, Jimmy would be against him. The boy would leave town in humiliation. It would rub his pride the wrong way and Jimmy would hate him and leave.

No, leave things as they are, Cal Rutherford. That warning washed against the edges of his mind. It was like lapping, muddy water—flood water. Laden with silt, dirty with mud—dirty as the deal the farmers were getting here on Puma Valley. *Things will work out all right, Cal Rutherford*.

They stopped, and looked down Puma City's main street. A narrow strip, straight and covered with dust; dust stirred by this wind that held the hint of rain. Cal gave it a long glance.

"Your rifle—it's loaded?"

"One in the barrel, Cal. Five shots in the magazine. All I have to do is pull back the hammer and fire."

Cal nodded.

"Maybe they won't fight. Maybe it isn't a gun shot Marfa Jordan's shoulder. Maybe a hoss has dumped him, or he has had an accident."

Cal said, "They'll fight. No matter what's wrong with Jordan, if I call them, they'll fight."

They stood there. The wind was insolent and it stirred dust. This dust swirled, came toward them, veered, and died. A woman came out of the Mercantile. Cal said, "Mrs. West."

"Where's Eddie?"

Cal said, "I don't know. Prob'ly in a store. I hope she stays out of the way until this is over."

"Jack Hutchinson," Jimmy said.

Hutchinson came out of the saloon. He

crossed the street, saw them, turned toward them. He rubbed his close-cropped moustache and looked at Jimmy Stephens' rifle. "Rabbit hunting?" he joked.

"Wild rabbits," Jimmy said.

Hutchinson got the rebuff, and Cal saw the indecision start at the man's mouth, rise and give his eyes color. Hutchinson said, "There's lots of them around," and turned and walked into the Merc. He looked back at the door, measuring them with a fine glance, and he looked again at Jimmy Stephens' rifle, and the railroad superintendent entered the store.

"I don't get him," Jimmy said quietly.

"Who does?"

Cal saw that John Shane still sat on the porch of the hotel. John Shane got up and looked at them and Cal saw him look at the swinging wide door of the Merc. that had just closed behind Jack Hutchinson. Shane stood there and looked back at them. Then he went into the hotel and Cal saw him cross the lobby for the stairway that led to the second floor. John Shane moved beyond the reach of the window and became lost from Cal's vision.

"Another funny bird I can't savvy," Jimmy said.

"Maybe he don't fit into this."

Jimmy shook his head. "He fits in somewhere. I can feel that in my bum hip." He showed his boyish smile.

Cal stood and kept watching. He ran his gaze up and down the street, gauging it for danger, hidden or open—he found neither. Evidently Pete Glenn and Marfa Jordan were still in the doctor's office.

He let his gaze rest on the office. The front door was closed. Jimmy noticed this, too.

"They're still in there, Cal. Otherwise the doc would have the door open again on a day this hot. He's a queer one, that doc. When he wants to be he can close his mouth as hard as a mud-turtle."

"They're in there!"

Jimmy looked at him. "What's the deal? You make the plans, Cal. You know this better'n I do."

Cal talked quietly. Marfa Jordan and Pete Glenn had gone in the back door of the doctor's office. That meant they wanted nobody to see them. Undoubtedly they would come out the rear door, too.

Jimmy nodded. "The alley, then?"

"The alley."

They crossed the street and went between two buildings and came to the alley behind the doctor's office. Beyond them the rear of the hotel jutted out and Cal thought he caught the glimpse of movement behind the curtains of a room. He gave the room attention and decided he had been wrong. The window was open and the wind ruffled the lace curtains, throwing deceptive shadows he might have mistaken for human movement.

Cal said, "You take that spot," and designated. Jimmy walked past the office-door and settled beside a garbage can and was silent. Cal looked for the broncs of Marfa Jordan and Pete Glenn. He went down the alley a few feet and looked into a shed. Two saddled horses were tied inside.

Bar N horses.

Cal came back, stride measured. He settled his back against a board fence and watched the door of the medico's office.

He waited.

17

DOC WILSON worked without asking questions. He had been too long in the cow-country to ask many questions. When he knew a man real well, he would unlimber and ask questions and joke, but he had to know a person real well to afford such liberties. And he did not know Marfa Jordan or Pete Glenn that well.

He recognized Jordan's wound as a bullet wound, but he made no mention of that fact. One time the county sheriff had asked him to notify him the minute he treated a bullet wound, but Doc Wilson had paid the order not the slightest attention. If a man wanted to get shot, or managed to shoot himself in an accident—well, that was his own business.

Too darned many laws anyway. Every time a man turned he broke a law. Now Doc Wilson washed the wound with something that stung and drew paleness into the rough jowls of Marfa Jordan.

"Won't hurt long."

Jordan grunted, "Hope not."

Pete Glenn sat on a chair and watched. "How bad, Doc?"

"Infection," the medico said. "We might stop it in time. You should have let me look at it right after it happened."

Marfa Jordan smiled. "I was in a hurry."

"How long till he'll be okay?"

Doc Wilson looked at him. "I'm not God. I can't control the future. You hire him for his gun, Glenn. He can still fire with his right hand."

"Don't get snuffy, pill-roller!"

Doc Wilson measured Pete Glenn with a long glance. The medico's lips had moved back and they held that position for some time before resuming their original shape. Then the medico, wordlessly, returned to Jordan's shoulder.

He probed, and his fingers brought grunts from Jordan. He washed the wound again, forcing the medicant into it, and finally he had it clean in his judgment. He then bound it with white bandages, chubby fingers working quickly and competently. He tied the bandage into place.

"Help me put on my shirt, Glenn?"

Glenn said, "The doc will help you, Marfa."

Glenn moved to the window and pulled the curtain to one side and looked into the alley. Marfa Jordan was on his feet, with Doc Wilson helping him put his bad arm into his shirt-sleeve. Glenn watched and Jordan watched Glenn, unconsciously struggling with the sleeve. Then Glenn let the curtain drop.

"No use putting on that shirt, Jordan."

Jordan stopped. "Why?"

Glenn looked at Doc Wilson, who stood silent, watching. Glenn said, "Cal Rutherford is out there leaning against that fence."

Surprise sucked color out of Marfa Jordan's face, leaving the whiskers black and shiny. He looked at Doc Wilson, whose face was without color or hope. Then he jerked his gaze back to Pete Glenn.

"Somebody's seen us come in that back door. They've run an' tol' Cal Rutherford." Marfa Jordan's tongue licked his bottom lip. "We can shoot through the window an' git him, Pete."

"I don't think so."

"Why not?"

Pete Glenn said quietly, "Look behind you!"

Jordan turned, ponderous yet quick. And what he saw drew his eyebrows down in wild anger. For Doc Wilson now held a rifle. A .30-30. And Doc had the rifle on them.

"No ambush from my office."

Glenn turned stormy. "You'll pay for this . . . later." Reason wiped anger away, chalk falling under a sponge on a slate. He went back to the window and raised the curtain and looked out. "He's alone, I guess."

"Jimmy Stephens?"

"Can't see him," Glenn said.

Glenn let the curtain drop. He stood and rubbed his jaw and this brought a smile to him. He seemed pleased with some inner jest. Marfa Jordan watched and realized he did not know Pete Glenn, nor would he ever really know him. The man was a riddle. He was the far wind, whining over sagebrush; he was the uncertain dance of sunlight, dark when it should have been dazzling. Marfa Jordan thought these thoughts and they drove a shaft of steel into him.

"Well, Glenn, the end is here."

"Good," Glenn said.

"No front door for us," Jordan said. He was sober now, the shock gone; he flexed his mighty right hand, limbering the fingers. He looked at Doc Wilson's rifle. "You can put that peashooter back into its genuine hardwood case now, Doc. Put it back into that felt-lined rack over there. If it went off and shot you, ain't no doc who could treat you." Cynicism and daring edged Marfa Jordan's voice. He was building himself up to the moment through the use of brave talk.

Doc Wilson said, "Get out!" He gestured with the rifle.

Pete Glenn said, "With pleasure. But we'll be back." He took the key from the door and inserted it on the outside of the latch. "You're not coming out this door to side your friend. And stay clear of windows or we'll kill you."

"This is no fight of mine."

Pete Glenn balanced that. He pushed it around, felt of it, judged it; he decided Doc Wilson was neutral. And that thought was good. The doc only wanted fair play. Pete Glenn said, "I give you my word, Doc. Marfa Jordan meets him . . . if he's alone. If there's more than him, I give my gun into it."

"Fair enough."

Jordan grinned. "Ol' Marfa gets the axe again." He kept moving his right hand, loosening his fingers, stretching them. Now that hand came to his gun and twisted it and lifted it so it would ride high.

"Jordan said, "Here we go!"

He almost ripped the door from its hinges. He slammed it back, and it rocked against the wall and finally steadied. Jordan stepped out and he went ahead, moving into the dust. He stopped and looked at Cal Rutherford. He looked at him with great steadiness, and in this levelness was a great quietness. The nervousness had left Jordan now. It had run out with a wildness, the moment the door rocked back; now he was calm and confident and sure of his ability.

Jordan glanced back. Pete Glenn stood on the steps of the doctor's office. Glenn stood there, and Glenn looked up and down the alley. Then Glenn said, "Jimmy Stephens, up there, Jordan!"

Marfa Jordan pulled back, as if stung by a wasp. He pushed back fast, running back, getting next to the wall. He did not want his back exposed. He looked, and in that stabbing glance, he saw Jimmy Stephens. The kid had a rifle. He had been hiding behind the big garbage-can.

"Two of them, Glenn."

Marfa Jordan spoke without emotion. A wind was rustling leaves, and this rustle had turned into words, and so sounded Marfa Jordan's voice to Cal Rutherford, who waited and was tight inside.

Glenn said, "Two of them. You still take Rutherford."

Marfa Jordan swung his gaze on Cal Rutherford. He watched him with the unblinking stare of a fat toad. He kept swinging his right hand, moving it in a short circle, and this grew smaller and smaller, centering around his gun's grip. Finally he asked, "What do you want, Rutherford?"

Cal Rutherford's voice sounded distant, even to himself. "You've got a wound in your shoulder, Jordan. The kid here saw you two sneak into the doc's office. I was wondering if that stray bullet that night didn't wound you?"

"What night?"

"When my granary was blasted."

Jordan looked at Pete Glenn. Glenn never took his eyes from Jimmy Stephens. Glenn caught the swift turn of his gunman's head.

"There's no use arguing, Jordan. They came for guns; they'll get them. Pull and fire an'—"

Those were Pete Glenn's last words. For his

gun rose, and Jimmy Stephens sent a rifle bullet through the heart of Pete Glenn. He did it with a short, jerking pull of his rifle, catching the sights as the rifle went up. He sent the bullet through Pete Glenn, and Glenn moved ahead. Glenn seemed surprised, and something loosened his lips. It loosened his fingers, too, and the smoking .45 fell down. Glenn mumbled something, or he tried to speak, but if he said a word, young Jimmy Stephens did not hear it. For Cal Rutherford and Marfa Jordan were firing.

Jimmy wheeled, rifle still raised. But he held fire. He watched it with an odd sort of detachment. He was part of this, he had done his share; luck had been with him. Glenn had got in one shot. Jimmy Stephens remembered the rise of dust, geyser-like and quick, beyond his boots.

He watched.

Later, he said it seemed years. It seemed to drag on and on and on, and each hour ripped something more out of him. Actually, it lasted only four shots. And each man got in two.

For Marfa Jordan's first bullet had sent Cal Rutherford back. It had smashed out of the day, hard and wicked, but it had been sent without aim, and it hit Cal in the ribs. It ripped along his left ribs and swung him. By that time, his own .45 was out.

Afterwards, Cal remembered with great clarity that wild moment; now, he was part of it, and he was cool. Pain was something detached, belonging to his ribs, yet not bothering him. He realized this was because he was under stress. He saw Glenn go down, and he saw the dim form of Jimmy Stephens. These were things beyond his limits, but they were still part of this.

His gun lifted, the barrel hot. Marfa Jordan screamed something and Cal thought, 'I've hit him!' There was no lift in this either. The fate of Puma Valley was being settled in this bleak strip of alley and its dust. This alley, lined by battered, rough out-buildings. There was irony there. Just as there was irony in the fact that Marfa Jordan's first shot had been too far to the right.

Jordan came ahead, walking ahead, and he shot the same time Cal shot. The fence ripped beside Cal and Jordan stopped. He looked at Cal, and Jordan's face was grave—torn with lines, torn by fear. And Jordan said, "Don't shoot again, Cal; don't shoot!"

Cal lifted his gun, hammer up. He looked and Jordan dropped his gun. Jordan got on his hands and knees and felt in the dust, searching for the gun. Cal watched, and a great loneliness was in him. Jordan felt and found the gun and tried to lift it. Then Jordan went on his belly. He sighed, and dust billowed from his breath —a small uncertain cloud claimed by the wind.

"We did it!" Jimmy screamed.

Cal moved ahead, and his knees fell down. He heard a rifle talk, and he felt a bullet hit his thigh. He realized this did not make sense. Glenn and Jordan were down, and Jimmy Stephens was coming toward him; and Jimmy would not shoot him. Then a man ran out of the alley.

He had been hiding in a shed. Bullets spouted dust around him as he ran for the street. Cal thought, That's odd. I'm not shootin'; neither is Jimmy. He looked and saw a rifle from the window of the hotel. It talked and talked, and he remembered the movement he'd seen behind that curtain.

"Eddie?" he asked.

Jimmy Stephens was beside him. "No, the fellow with the rifle was John Shane. He downed Hutchinson out in the street."

"You got me," Jimmy said. "I don't savvy it. Hutchinson must be in with them. He shot to kill you from hidin'. Shane saved your life. Hey, Cal—"

Cal was out.

John Shane said, "I'm a railroad detective. I always work on the quiet. I wouldn't take my own mother in my confidence. Hutchinson saw a chance to grab some easy land that will be worth a lot of money in a few years."

Cal said, "He worked with Glenn?"

Shane nodded. Doc Wilson said, "Roll over a little, Cal, an' let me get this bandage under you. I got your hip bandaged. You'll be in bed two weeks, anyway. Jimmy, grab this end of the bandage!"

Jimmy kissed Cal on the cheek. "We got out lucky, pal."

Cal asked, "Glenn an' Jordan?"

Doc Wilson said, "You two did a good job. Farmers have headed out to clean out the Bar N. But I'll bet by the time they get there word has gone out an' the ranch is deserted. Them hired Bar N gun-hands won't fight with Jordan and Glenn gone."

"Hope you're, right," Cal said.

Cal felt sick. He closed his eyes. He listened to John Shane's voice. "Hutchinson ain't dead. He's down the depot, an' he's talked plenty. Glenn backed him. Hutchinson led some of the Bar N men when Jimmy an' his grain-tank got waylaid."

"He aimed to help Glenn an' Jordan?"

"He did. But I watched him from upstairs. He intercepted those letters you wrote to the railroad officials. They all had to go through him, remember? The officials got worried and sent me out. They've got money to lend you and your farmers, Cal."

Cal asked, "Then everything is okay?"

"All fine as frog's hair, Cal. You did a good job. I would have acted before, but I didn't have direct evidence that would hold in court."

Jimmy went to the door. "We'll be out in a minute," he told somebody.

Cal felt good, despite his wounds. He opened his eyes. "Who you talkin' to out there?"

Doc Wilson stepped back. "Well, we got him looking like a mummy." He looked at John Shane. "You've told him enough for one session. You an' me an' Jimmy are skeedaddlin' out of here."

"Why?"

Cal got no answer. Doc Wilson left, followed by Shane and Jimmy. Soon the door opened. Eddie Malone came in.

"Cal!"

"Eddie!"

The sunlight danced on her golden hair. Cal thought, It'll run out of gold some day and show silver. And he'd be around to watch it change. That was the main thing, the essential thing.

"Cal, it's raining ten miles away. The depot operator just got it over his wire. Cal, it'll save crops. Cal—"

She was kneeling-beside him. Cal ran his fingers through her red-gold hair and brought her head down to his. Then both were silent for a long time.

FIGHTING RAMROD
by Charles N. Heckelmann

Most men would have cut their losses, but Frazer counted the bullets in his guns and said he'd soak the range in blood before he'd give up another inch of what was his.

LONE GUN
by Eric Allen

Smoke Blackbird had been away too long. The Lequires had seized the Blackbird farm, forcing the Indians and settlers off, and no one seemed willing to fight! He had to fight alone.

THE THIRD RIDER
by Barry Cord

Mel Rawlins wasn't going to let anything stand in his way. His father was murdered, his two brothers gone. Now Mel rode for vengeance.

RIDE A LONE TRAIL
by Gordon D. Shirreffs

The valley was about to explode into open range war. All it needed was the fuse and Ken Macklin was it.

ARIZONA DRIFTERS
by W. C. Tuttle

When drifting Dutton and Lonnie Steelman decide to become partners they find that they have a common enemy in the formidable Thurston brothers.

TOMBSTONE
by Matt Braun

Wells Fargo paid Luke Starbuck to outgun the silver-thieving stagecoach gang at Tombstone. Before long Luke can see the only thing bearing fruit in this eldorado will be the gallows tree.

HIGH BORDER RIDERS
by Lee Floren

Buckshot McKee and Tortilla Joe cut the trail of a border tough who was running Mexican beef into Texas. They stopped the smuggler in his tracks.

HARD MAN WITH A GUN
by Charles N. Heckelmann

After Bob Keegan lost the girl he loved and the ranch he had sweated blood to build, he had nothing left but his guts and his guns but he figured that was enough.

BRETT RANDALL, GAMBLER
by E. B. Mann

Larry Day had the choice of running away from the law or of assuming a dead man's place. No matter what he decided he was bound to end up dead.

THE GUNSHARP
by William R. Cox

The Eggerleys weren't very smart. They trained their sights on Will Carney and Arizona's biggest blood bath began.

THE DEPUTY OF SAN RIANO
by Lawrence A. Keating and
Al. P. Nelson

When a man fell dead from his horse, Ed Grant was spotted riding away from the scene. The deputy sheriff rode out after him and came up against everything from gunfire to dynamite.

SUNDANCE: IRON MEN
by Peter McCurtin

Sundance, assigned to save the railroad from a murder spree, soon came to realise that he'd have to fight fire with fire, bullets with bullets and death with death!

FARGO: MASSACRE RIVER
by John Benteen

Fargo spurred his horse to the edge of the road. The ambushers up ahead had now blocked the road. Fargo's convoy was a jumble, a perfect target for the insurgents' weapons!

SUNDANCE:
DEATH IN THE LAVA
by John Benteen

The land echoed with the thundering hoofs of Modoc ponies. In minutes they swooped down and captured the wagon train and its cargo of gold. But now the halfbreed they called Sundance was going after it, and he swore nothing would stand in his way.

GUNS OF FURY
by Ernest Haycox

Dane Starr, alias Dan Smith, wanted to close the door on his past and hang up his guns, but people wouldn't let him. Good men wanted him to settle their scores for them. Bad men thought they were faster and itched to prove it. Starr had to keep killing just to stay alive.

FARGO: PANAMA GOLD
by John Benteen

Cleve Buckner was recruiting an army of killers, gunmen and deserters from all over Central America. With foreign money behind him, Buckner was going to destroy the Panama Canal before it could be completed. Fargo's job was to stop Buckner—and to eliminate him once and for all!

FARGO: THE SHARPSHOOTERS
by John Benteen

The Canfield clan, thirty strong, were raising hell in Texas. One of them had shot a Texas Ranger, and the Rangers had to bring in the killer. Fargo was tough enough to hold his own against the whole clan.

SUNDANCE: OVERKILL
by John Benteen

Sundance's reputation as a fighting man had spread. There was no job too tough for the halfbreed to handle. So when a wealthy banker's daughter was kidnapped by the Cheyenne, he offered Sundance $10,000 to rescue the girl.

HELL RIDERS
by Steve Mensing

Wade Walker's kid brother, Duane, was locked up in the Silver City jail facing a rope at dawn. Wade was a ruthless outlaw, but he was smart, and he had vowed to have his brother out of jail before morning!

DESERT OF THE DAMNED
by Nelson Nye

The law was after him for the murder of a marshal—a murder he didn't commit. Breen was after him for revenge—and Breen wouldn't stop at anything . . . blackmail, a frameup . . . or murder.

DAY OF THE COMANCHEROS
by Steven C. Lawrence

Their very name struck terror into men's hearts—the Comancheros, a savage army of cutthroats who swept across Texas, leaving behind a bloodstained trail of robbery and murder.